≠
L719s

Shanny on Her Own

Shanny on Her Own

by
LAEL LITTKE

HARCOURT BRACE JOVANOVICH, PUBLISHERS
San Diego   New York   London

LIBRARY OF CONGRESS CATALOGING IN PUBLICATION DATA

Littke, Lael.
   Shanny on her own.

   Summary: Fifteen-year-old Shannon learns a great deal about herself and life in general while spending the summer in the country with an elderly aunt.
   [1. Self-acceptance—Fiction.
2. Country life—Fiction.
3. Friendship—Fiction]
I. Title.
PZ7.L719Sh   1985   [Fic]   85-8451
ISBN 0-15-273531-3

Designed by Michael Farmer
Printed in the United States of America
First edition
A B C D E

For George, my husband

Shanny on Her Own

1

I knew all along that Thor Jorgensen would be a wimp. I mean, Aunt Adabelle's letters were too enthusiastic about him. "You'll like Thor," she had written right after Mom and Dad arranged to inter me for a month at her ranch in Idaho. "He works for me when I need him, and he'll introduce you to all the other nice young folks here."

Then in parentheses she had added, "The girls around here tell me Thor has S.A."

I assumed that meant Sex Appeal. Aunt Adabelle has a habit of abbreviating words she doesn't feel comfortable writing out in full. Sometimes her letters look as if they're in secret code.

In her next letter Aunt Adabelle wrote, "Thor will meet you at the bus station in Pratt. You're going to like him, Shanny."

If there's anything I've learned in my fifteen years, it's that when somebody tries too hard to sell you something, you'd better examine the merchandise. Like this whole deal at Aunt Adabelle's ranch. I was supposed to go there to help her get ready to move into a retirement home. Mom and Dad gave me a super snow job about how much I would love it there, but I knew it was all just part of their project to Shape Up Shanny. It was supposed to get me started on the road to making something of myself. "Shanny is searching for who she is," Mom was always saying to explain why I did the things I did. Like the Great Dog-Food Caper, for which I was supposed to be overwhelmed with guilt and want to change into a worthwhile person with goals and ambitions. Going to the ranch on my own was supposed to change my life.

Never mind that I didn't want my life changed. Forget that I already had goals and ambitions, which at the moment were to spend my summer days at the beach with my best friend Flame Ferguson, plotting how to meet the lifeguard with the dragon tattooed on his chest.

Besides, that dog-food caper was not my fault. Not entirely, anyway. At least it wasn't my idea. Well, part of it wasn't.

But what did it matter? Here I was on the bus, staring out at the city of Pratt—all two blocks of it. It just goes to show you how much power I have, how much control over my own life. Zilch, that's how much.

I sighed as I looked out at the Sprouse Reitz Variety Store and the O. P. Skaggs Market. Nothing like a Woolworth's or a Safeway in good old Pratt. The only familiar thing in the whole town was the movie theater marquee, which announced that it was running *E.T.* Appropriate, I thought. I wanted to call home, too.

2

Up ahead I could see some people waiting in front of the squatty Pratt Hotel, which I assumed also served as a bus station since that was where we were headed. Suddenly a thought hit me. What if Thor turned out to be something like the big deal Norse god he was named after? What if I was mistaken about his wimphood? Was I ready?

Hurriedly I shifted my eyes to look at my reflection in the glass of the window, making a quick check of my assets.

Just before I left home, Flame had given me a short, jagged haircut, leaving a thin tail of long hair at the nape of my neck. She had dyed the tail purple. My eye shadow was the same color, and so was the fake jewel I had glued to my left nostril. In contrast, the three tiny gold earrings attached to three little holes pierced in my right earlobe were very understated. A charcoal gray ragbag blouse, which drooped off my left shoulder, and a long-ish khaki-colored skirt over fishnet stockings and high-heeled go-go boots completed my ensemble.

I looked just right.

"Fight back," Flame had told me. "Don't go there meekly looking for yourself. Show them who you are right off, and pretty soon you'll be back here in the fast lane."

Lifting my chin, I glared out of the window, ready to face Thor Jorgensen.

And there he was, standing on the street along with a couple of women in light summer dresses. He was wiping his eyeglasses on his flowered necktie as he watched the bus pull in. He wore scuffed cowboy boots, blue jeans, and a blue shirt with the flowered necktie

3

that doubled as an eyeglass cleaner. He had freckles and a spray of red hair. A razor nick on his chin announced that he had scraped off a little fuzz for this big occasion. Without his glasses, he squinted a lot.

If Thor Jorgensen had Sex Appeal, it had taken the day off.

With another sigh, I yanked my duffel bag from the rack overhead and struggled along the narrow aisle with it. The rest of my stuff, my drums and books, were in the baggage compartment.

Getting off the bus, I walked over to Thor. "Hi," I said. "I'll be ready as soon as I get my drums."

He hooked his glasses behind his ears and stared at me. His eyes were owly behind the thick lenses.

"Ready for what?" he whispered. His Adam's apple tripped up and down his neck like a fast elevator.

"I'm Shanny. You're supposed to pick me up."

Looking horrified, he backed away from me. "I don't pick up girls."

I followed him. "Aren't you going to take me to Aunt Adabelle's ranch?"

The guy shook his head so hard that he almost whipped his glasses off his face. "I'm going to take the bus to Pocatello to visit my grandmother." He continued to back away from me, and I could see that in about one second he was going to fall over a couple of suitcases that must have belonged to the women in the summer dresses.

"Hey, stop!" I yelled, just as the back of his knees touched the suitcases. He started to topple. I made a lunge for him, thinking I'd save him from a fall. It was

4

too late, and we both plunged to the sidewalk, my arms wrapped tightly around his waist.

"My word," said one of the women, "I wish we'd dared go after them like that when *I* was a girl."

The guy lay stiffly on the street, his arms straight along his sides. I was on top of him, nose to nose.

"Pardon me, but who I'm looking for is Thor Jorgensen. Do you know where I can find him?"

A pickup truck skidded to a stop behind the bus. It was dark blue with a big silver lightning bolt painted across its door.

"*That's* Thor," the guy on the ground said. "*I'm* DeWitt Horspool." His eyes closed. "Thank God," he whispered.

Thor got out of the truck and came toward us while I tried to untangle myself from DeWitt. When I looked up and saw him, I knew this was a moment that would divide time forever for me. From now on I would think of everything in my life as happening B.T. or A.T.—Before Thor or After Thor.

Thor was every girl's dream come true, in blue jeans, cowboy boots, and a yellow T-shirt that advertised John Deere Farm Machinery. Exactly the kind of guy to help a girl find herself.

But was I really the kind of girl he would look at? Dear God, I prayed suddenly, give me long blond hair and blue eyes with lashes that sweep the street. I'll try out for cheerleader and even learn to sew, if You'll just make me that kind of girl.

I had new respect for Aunt Adabelle. She told it like it was. Thor had enough S.A. to make a living selling the surplus to guys like DeWitt Horspool.

5

"Wow," I whispered. I climbed off DeWitt's chest and sprang to my feet, reaching down a hand to help him up. Ignoring it, he scrambled to an upright position by himself.

"I was just trying to help," I said.

DeWitt dusted off his clothes with both hands. "Help *him*," he said, pointing at Thor and running for the bus.

"Hey, DeWitt," Thor called after him, "how long you going to be gone? We have a rehearsal Saturday, you know."

DeWitt paused in the doorway of the bus. "I was only going for a couple of days." He looked at me. "But maybe I'll stay longer." He disappeared inside the bus.

The door whooshed shut, and the bus left.

Thor turned to me. "You're Shannon."

I was pleased that he knew me. "How did you know?" He grinned.

I knew how he knew. Mom must have phoned Aunt Adabelle to tell her what to expect. I could almost hear her telling it. "Shanny is . . . unusual," she would have said. Mom is always kind. She would never say freaky.

"Unusual—right?" I said to Thor.

His grin widened. "I think the word was 'different.'"

I whinnied flirtatiously. "So how could you tell that I was 'different?'"

Thor scratched his head in a fake-puzzled way, scuffing the toe of one boot in the dust like the bashful cowboys in Western movies. "Don't rightly know, ma'am, unless it was the way you were sitting astride old DeWitt Horspool." He laughed, remembering. It was a great big hooty, *friendly* kind of laugh.

6

He liked me! Just the way I was, he liked me! Had I already found myself?

Cancel the blond hair, I instructed God, happy that I wouldn't have to learn to sew after all.

"Well, anyway, I'm Thor Jorgensen." He stuck out his hand.

Just touching it made my heart whiz around in my chest.

"I would have guessed from the thunderbolt on your truck."

His face brightened. "Oh, so you know about the great god Thor."

"Sure. Mythology is my thing."

Actually, it's Trivia that's my thing. Flame and I have a collection of what we call Esoteric Facts. We read a lot of different things, and we keep a file of facts. Flame says that's the way to be popular because if we're at a party and the conversation stops dead, we can throw out an Esoteric Fact or two to get things started again. She says we'll always be in demand for parties, but we haven't been invited to one since the time Flame got carried away right while we were eating and described how the ancient Egyptians prepared bodies for mummification.

"Not too many people know about Norse gods," Thor said. He looked impressed. "Well, let's get your stuff loaded up. Aunt Adabelle is expecting you for supper. Where are your suitcases?"

"This is it." I hoisted my duffel bag to my shoulder.

Thor took it from me and tossed it into the back of his truck. "Is this all?"

So how much baggage do you need for a guilt trip? I was there to be reformed, not to put on a fashion show.

"That's it, except for my drums and books." I nodded toward the stack of books I'd tied together with twine and the parts of my drum set, all zippered up in their brown canvas cases.

"Drums?" Thor walked over to my stuff. "I don't believe this."

Suddenly I was embarrassed. How could I explain to Thor, or to anyone else for that matter, why I had lugged my drums with me? How could anyone else understand how I could pull my world together by roosting in my nest of drums and cutting loose with a volley of sound?

"I should have left them at home," I said apologetically.

"No, this is great." Thor practically danced around my drums. "We're doing road shows this summer, and we don't have anybody in town who plays the drums. Shanny, you're a Genuine Certified Miracle!"

I didn't have a clue as to what he was talking about. It probably had something to do with whatever they were rehearsing that Thor wanted DeWitt Horspool to come back for.

It didn't matter, so long as Thor thought I was wonderful. His words flowed over me like cool water on a blistering hot day. I felt as if the whole world were suddenly unreal. I planned what I would write to Flame that night. "It's like a romantic movie," I would say, "and I'm Scarlett O'Hara!"

In a glow I picked up my stack of books while Thor stowed my drums in the back of his pickup. He carried them as if they were fragile eggs, arranging them in the truck bed so they didn't bump against one another.

"They survived all right so far," I told him. "They travel pretty well in those canvas covers."

"Don't want to take any chances." Thor helped me into the cab of the truck with as much care as he took with the drums.

I loved it. I hoped the trip to Aunt Adabelle's ranch would take hours. Days! She lives in a place called Wolf Creek, which is several miles from Pratt. It was going to be wonderful, riding in that cozy truck, just Thor and me.

Thor got in on the driver's side and started the engine. "What's with all the big books? Are you planning to learn everything you always wanted to know this summer?"

I had brought my paperback copies of volumes one and two of *The People's Almanac* with me, as well as *Bulfinch's Mythology* and a book entitled *Mysteries of the Unexplained* that Flame had given me for my birthday. I had also brought ten issues of *National Geographic*. Flame had advised me to take along plenty of reading material. "They probably won't have TV way out there in Idaho," she had said, "or maybe not even electricity. Take something along to keep your mind from totaling out."

I didn't see any reason to give Thor direct quotes, so I just said, "I like to read a lot."

Thor nodded. "So do I."

I chalked up another point for me on my mental scoreboard. Finding myself here was going to be a cinch.

Thor turned the truck back down the main street of Pratt and parked in front of the O. P. Skaggs Market. I supposed he had to pick up groceries. That was all right. I would do a mental instant replay of the past ten minutes while I waited.

"Be right back." Thor opened his door and jumped out.

Fondly I watched him run inside the store and come out a few minutes later loaded down with bags and groceries.

And followed by a girl.

The long blond hair I had prayed for a few minutes earlier was on this girl's head. She also had soft brown eyes and terrific legs that sort of twinkled when she walked, if you know what I mean. She wore dark blue walking shorts with a lighter blue T-shirt, and she made the whole street more interesting just by being there.

My heart fell somewhere down around my knees as I watched her. I should have known a guy like Thor would come fully equipped with a girl friend.

Thor put the groceries in the back of the truck, then came to my door and opened it. "Shanny," he said, "this is Twyla Starbuck. She's the one who painted the thunderbolt here on the door. Twyla, this is Shannon Alder. She's going to be staying with Aunt Adabelle Spencer for the summer."

Twyla lifted those soft brown eyes to mine. "I'm happy to meet you, Shannon," she said. She looked a little startled.

"Call me Shanny," I mumbled from under the wreckage of my fantasy summer. I slid over to make room for Twyla.

She just stood there. It was when Thor began to get a little red-faced that I realized I was in Twyla's place. Dumb, stupid me. Mentally I scrubbed off the points I had chalked up for myself. I scrambled out of the truck, catching the hem of my skirt on the gearshift as I did so. At least three inches of it ripped loose and drooped behind me as I stood there wishing I could disappear. Twyla climbed in and scooted over to the middle of the seat.

I got in next to her. As Thor closed the door, I caught a glimpse of myself in the glass of the window. My hair stuck up in spikes, and the sun glinted off my nose jewel.

Was this really the Real Me?

Oh, God, I prayed again, about that blond hair . . .

2

My father is a pickle. He does commercials on TV, and right now he's doing a whole series of them for a pickle company. He's very good at what he does, probably because he says it's just as hard to be a convincing pickle as it is to be a believable Hamlet, so he really works at it. He says whatever part you play, you have to create a mental image of yourself as that character, then project that image to your audience.

I decided to create a mental image of myself as cool and beautiful and desirable and project that image to Thor. It was hard, though, to project it past Twyla since she was sitting between us.

But then maybe I could be more convincing if he couldn't see me. So I sat quietly with a nice smile, which is what Twyla was doing.

Nobody said anything as we drove out of town. Thor, who had been quite talkative when we were alone in the truck, didn't seem to have anything to say now.

Twyla turned and smiled at me a couple of times, giving me the full benefit of a set of teeth that could have had their own TV commercial. But she didn't say anything, either.

Finally Thor cleared his throat. "Shanny's from Los Angeles," he told Twyla.

"Oh." Twyla said the single word sympathetically as if being from Los Angeles was some kind of disease. "Did you take the bus all the way from there?" She gave me a nice smile.

Around *my* nice smile I said, "No, I flew as far as Salt Lake City."

"All by yourself?"

"No, on an airplane." My smile dripped sugar.

Twyla's smile wavered, but Thor laughed and leaned around her to grin at me. Twyla leaned forward and said, "Why, look how high the alfalfa is."

I looked out at the fields on either side of us before I realized that Twyla wasn't interested in alfalfa. She was just blocking Thor's view of me.

We rode in silence for another mile. Then Thor said, "This is a great year to come for a visit, Shanny. Besides the road shows, we're having a Pioneer Day rodeo."

Twyla smiled at me again. "Maybe you'd like to try out for Pioneer Day Queen, Shanny. All the girls do."

I imagined a long line of Twyla clones. I pictured me somewhere in that line.

I wondered if Twyla was being sarcastic. But her brown eyes, which took up all the face space not occupied by her teeth, were innocent.

"My mom was Pioneer Day Queen one year when she stayed with Aunt Adabelle," I said.

13

"Really?" Twyla looked as if she wondered how any-body who had produced me had ever been Pioneer Day Queen.

Actually, my mom is very pretty. And she liked being Pioneer Day Queen. She rates things by Goose Bumps, and she says being queen was a ten G.B. occasion. She has pictures of herself in an old-fashioned white dress sprigged with blue flowers, and a sunbonnet perched on her flowing blond hair. "Cascading" is the word my dad uses. "There she was," he says, "with her eyes as blue as the flowers on her dress and her yellow hair cascading down across her shoulders."

Dad says that's when he fell in love with Mom.

For just a moment I let myself think of *me* dressed in a pioneer dress, riding on a float made to look like a covered wagon, which is what Mom rode on. Thor would be there gazing at me, and years later he would tell our children about it: "There she was, her nose jewel catch-ing the rays of the sun and her tail of purple hair wisping down her back."

It didn't seem the same.

I could dye my brown hair blond, like Mom's, but it would be a long time before it was going to cascade anywhere.

Besides, if I were just another clone in the long line of Twylas, who was going to see me?

Flame was right. Why was I trying to create a whole new Shanny? What I should do was *show* them who I was. Thor had liked me all right back there in Pratt when we first met. He had *liked* me "different."

Hitching myself forward so I could see both Twyla and Thor, I said, "Did you know that when chewing gum was patented back in 1869, a doctor claimed that it would make your intestines stick together?"

Twyla gave me a startled look and moved an inch closer to Thor.

"That's interesting, Shanny," Thor said. "Is that in those big books you brought with you?"

I nodded. "Did you know that in 1471 a chicken was accused of being a witch because she laid a colored egg? She was burned at the stake."

"You're a walking encyclopedia," Thor said. "Did you know, Twyla, that Shanny plays the drums and even brought her own set with her?"

For the first time Twyla looked enthusiastic. "Really? That's great. We'll win for sure."

Some day I would find out what they were talking about. It was enough right then to realize that it was my drums, not my wished-for cascading blond hair, that would make Big Points with the people in Wolf Creek— including Thor.

I pictured myself on stage in my nest of drums, with people milling around yelling, "Shanny won it for us." And Thor would whisper again, "Shanny, you really *are* a Genuine Certified Miracle."

"Shanny," Thor said, "you and DeWitt Horspool are going to be a fan*tas*tic team."

DeWitt! Thor was teaming me up with DeWitt!

I wondered if DeWitt was going to feel any better about that bit of news than I did.

It took us about half an hour to get to Aunt Adabelle's ranch in Wolf Creek. For the last few miles before we got there, we had been following a road that wound through a narrow valley alongside a wandering creek.

"That must be Wolf Creek," I commented during a dry spell in the conversation. It didn't seem the time for another fact.

"That's Chokecherry Creek," Thor said. "My family and Aunt Adabelle live on Chokecherry Creek. Twyla lives over on Sheep Creek."

I was confused. "Why is the town called Wolf Creek then?"

"Maybe it should have been called Three Creeks," Thor said. "Wolf Creek is the largest of the three, so I guess that's why the early pioneers named the town after it. I'll take you on a tour in a day or two, Shanny. I'll show you Klondike and Capital Hill and Out Town, where the church and blacksmith shop and cemetery are."

"We can show her Schoolhouse Hill and the ball park, too," Twyla said.

It was clear that she was reminding me—and Thor—that we wouldn't be going any place without her. Good old Twyla. She might be sweet and nice, but she was an expert at defending her turf.

Just then we came to a mailbox in the shape of a red barn with "Adabelle Spencer" printed across it in fancy letters.

"Twyla does calligraphy," Thor said, pointing at the mailbox. "She did that for Aunt Adabelle."

Busy little soul, that Twyla.

Thor turned into a long driveway that led down a slight hill and across a stone bridge that spanned Chokecherry Creek. Up ahead on a steep hillside I saw a tiny house. It wasn't much bigger than the metal lawn shed

Dad had put up in our back yard the summer before to hold the lawn mower and garden stuff. Its two dark windows stared down at us.

Flame was right again. Forget TV and telephones and all the good things of life. I'd be lucky if that house even had indoor plumbing.

"Aunt Adabelle's house is kind of small," I said.

Thor laughed. "That's not her house. Well, I mean it's hers, but it isn't the main house."

"That's the Bride's House," Twyla said in her soft little voice. It sounded romantic, the way she said it, and I looked back up there at the little house.

"That's the house Aunt Adabelle came to as a new bride almost sixty years ago," Thor went on. "She keeps it almost the same as it was then, and she spends a lot of time there, especially since Uncle Vic died about four years ago."

"I've been noticing that you call her *Aunt* Adabelle," I said. "Is she *your* aunt, too?" I hoped not. That would be the pits if Thor and I were related or something.

Thor shook his head. "Everybody calls her that. She's everybody's aunt. She never had any children of her own, you know."

I knew. If she had, I wouldn't have been there. Her own grandchildren would have come to pry her off her ranch, and I would have been back on the California beaches, searching for Shanny among the golden bodies that littered the warm sand.

But then of course I wouldn't have met Thor. Every cloud has a silver lining, as my mom says.

"She's actually my grandaunt," I said. "She's my grandmother's sister. I haven't even seen her since she

17

came to California to visit us when I was six years old."

"You'll like her," Thor said, and I remembered that was what she had said about him. She had been right. I did like Thor. And I was prepared to like her, not just because of that but also because we had something in common, she and I. We were both being uprooted from our own space.

I pictured her now, pottering about her little country kitchen, baking cookies or some other goody to welcome me.

Thor drove around a clump of trees, and I saw the "main house," as he had called it. It was a tall, skinny white house with an enormous porch wrapped around it like the label on a can. It sat in a bed of bright-colored flowers, surrounded by soft green lawn. There was a TV antenna sticking up from one of its gables.

I was relieved to know I would have some contact with the world. I'd even probably be able to see my dad on TV.

Thor stopped the truck in the big yard that separated the house from the red barn that was an oversize version of the mailbox we had just seen. But at least Twyla hadn't done any fancy writing on this one.

Thor got out and came around to open the door on my side. He put his hand up to help me out, which was the first time anybody had ever done that for me. I haven't gone out with a lot of guys, but when Woody Fenton took me to the wrestling matches at school, he was halfway into the gym before he realized that the passenger door on his old clunker was wired shut and I couldn't get out.

As I held Thor's hand and tried to step gracefully

down, I caught the heel of my go-go boot in the torn hem of my skirt. Off balance, I clutched at Thor, hopping around like a one-legged hen.

Twyla was out of the truck in a flash. "Here, let me help you, Shanny," she said.

I wondered if she was just being nice or if she was telling me to keep my sticky hands off her guy. But did she really have any claim on him? I didn't see TWYLA branded across his forehead in fancy calligraphy. Aunt Adabelle would have mentioned it if he was all staked out already, wouldn't she? She certainly wouldn't have said he had S.A. if he belonged to somebody else. I mean, you don't advertise something after it's taken.

"I'll unload your stuff, Shanny," Thor said when I was able to get both feet on the ground.

My torn hem dragged behind me, and I wished I didn't have to stand next to Twyla's cool perfection.

Thor had most of my gear unloaded when we heard a commotion from the red barn.

"You sly-eyed, bloat-bellied, mangy old coyote," screeched an angry voice. "Move your smelly carcass, or I'll nail it to the wall."

A horse exploded from the barn. He was speckled gray and skinny, a collection of sharp strung-together bones covered over by a coat of rough horsehide that sagged as if it were a couple sizes too big for him. He did a stiff-legged dance across the yard, his head down and his back arched.

"Blastoff!" Twyla exclaimed.

I thought she was doing a little ladylike cussing until she went on to say, "Blastoff's loose!" She sidled toward the open door of the truck.

19

A woman, tall and skinny and gray like the old horse, came striding from the barn followed by a kid in faded bib overalls.

"Catch him," the kid yelled when he saw Thor. "Don't let him get away."

The woman didn't seem concerned. "Good riddance," she said. "Let the old bandit go."

Aunt Adabelle? I didn't remember much about her from the one time I had seen her, but somehow I had the impression from Mom and The Cousins that she would be all bent over and frail and *old*.

Now wasn't the time to think about that, what with that horse plunging around the yard. Thor was running toward him, flapping his arms and yelling, "Hah! Hah!" The horse flung up his head, lifting his flabby upper lip in a sneer. But he kept coming, swinging his big ugly head from side to side.

Suddenly I saw that he was on a collision course with my drums. In about twenty more steps he was going to put one of his boat-sized feet right through the skin of my bass drum.

I froze. I wanted to join Twyla in the cab of the truck. But what if the horse ruined my drums? Without my drums I was no longer a Genuine Certified Miracle. Without them I had no chance of making Big Points with Thor. Without them I was nowhere.

"Scat!" I shrieked, flailing my arms and leaping toward my drums. "Heel! Stay!" What do you say to a horse? The only horses I knew were the wooden ones on the carousel at the Santa Monica pier.

Blastoff charged on like a tank, with Thor yelling at him from behind.

I had reached my stack of books. Tearing a *National Geographic* from under the twine, I flung it at the horse. "Stop!" I wailed.

The magazine hissed harmlessly past Blastoff. Its pages opened, and it fluttered to the ground like a wounded bird.

"Whoa!" I whispered hopelessly, finally locating some horse language in my memory banks.

Blastoff skidded to a stop, his head turned toward the dead *National Geo.* Blowing softly through his nose, he extended his skinny neck to peer at the magazine through milky eyes. He pushed at it with his nose. Opening his big lips, he picked it up and tasted it, then dropped it back in the dirt, expressing his opinion of it with another sneer.

I was afraid he was going to go berserk again and stomp my drums, and maybe me along with them. Yanking another *National Geographic* from my stack of books, I walked up and whacked him across the face with it. "Beat it!" I commanded.

Blastoff blinked. Pricking his ears forward, he looked at me. Stretching his skinny neck, he sniffed.

I wondered if he could bite me to death.

But the big horse merely lifted his lip again and turned to amble nonchalantly toward the corral, which extended out from the barn.

"Good show, Shanny!" Thor said as he followed the horse, closing the corral gate after he had gone inside.

Aunt Adabelle and the kid in the faded overalls hurried over to where I stood trembling.

"Wow!" the kid breathed. "Wow, I never saw a girl before who wasn't scared of Blastoff." He walked around

21

me, looking at me from all angles. "Wow," he said again.

I tried to look brave, as if I deserved his praise.

"You must be Shanny," Aunt Adabelle said. Putting her arms around me, she gave me a big hug, then held me away from her. "I had a better welcome planned, but I'm right glad you're here."

Up close, Aunt Adabelle looked older than she did from a distance. Her skin was like crumpled tissue paper, and her blue shirt and jeans didn't fit her thin body much better than Blastoff's hide fit him.

"It's been quite a trip," I said.

Thor came running back. "That was really gutsy, Shanny. You handled that old nag like a real pro. Wasn't she great?" He looked around at Aunt Adabelle and the kid while I blushed with pleasure. "You must own horses down there in Los Angeles," he finished.

"No," I said, "but I'm around horses a lot." I thought of the carousel and wondered if I should add, "Around and around and around." But why wipe out a good thing? I loved the admiration in Thor's eyes. It was a ten Goose-Bump occasion.

"I didn't dare rush up and grab him," Thor said, "because I was afraid it would make him barge right into your drums."

"She didn't even squeal or faint or nothing," the kid said.

Thor put his hand on the kid's hair. "This is my brother Bucky." Lowering his head, he whispered, "Hey, Buck, what did I tell you about messing around with that old meat grinder? You could get mangled."

Bucky hung his head briefly, then looked up at me.

"I bet she could ride him, couldn't she, Thor? I mean, she wasn't even afraid of him."

"She probably could." There was respect in Thor's voice.

I could have ridden a tornado at that moment if it would have kept Thor looking at me the way he was.

A whole lot of good it did me, though. After he carried my stuff into the house, he left with Twyla. If he liked gutsy women so much, why didn't he dump her and stay with me? She had hidden out in the truck cab during the whole scene with the old horse. But Thor went.

Bucky stayed. As he and Aunt Adabelle and I went into the house, he circled me again. I wished I had pinned up my dragging hem.

After another circle-around, Bucky took my hand and looked up at me with shining eyes. "You're the prettiest girl I ever saw, Shanny," he said.

When I wrote to Flame that night, I told her I had already met three guys and that one of them was in love with me.

I didn't tell her he was only eight years old.

3

I didn't sleep too well that night. It was strange being there in the same room, the same bed, that my mother had slept in when she was my age and had stayed with Aunt Adabelle. There was one difference then. The Cousins, daughters of Aunt Adabelle's brothers and sisters, had been there, too. But I was all alone. The old house kind of creaked and groaned, and I got a little scared because I heard some odd thumpings outside, too. But when I got up and looked out into the moonlit night, I saw it was only that old horse, Blastoff, thudding around the corral. His head was up, and every now and then he would fling out his back feet in a stiff kick. It was somehow comforting to know he was out there, awake, sort of like a watchdog.

I got back into bed and read an article in one of my *National Geographic*s about the salt marshes of the East Coast until I fell asleep.

I asked Aunt Adabelle about Thor the next day. I

mean, I didn't come right out and *ask*. I just started talking, kind of aiming toward what I wanted to find out, which was if Thor was all tied up with Twyla. I kept my voice low because Bucky was in the living room watching "All My Children" on TV, and I didn't want him to hear.

"I guess it's a good thing I brought my drums with me," I began as I set the table for dinner at noon. Aunt Adabelle said that's the way it was here at the ranch. You ate dinner at noon, then had supper at night after the chores were done. I hadn't gotten up in time for breakfast, so I didn't know how *it* worked, but I guess lunch just disappeared entirely. "Thor says they need drums for some kind of show," I went on.

"The road show." Aunt Adabelle was standing at the stove, stirring something in a big white enamel pot. "Oh my, yes, I'd say they might be right worked up about having some drums this year. Most years all we've had is a piano, with maybe R. G. Cole's tuba. But now with DeWitt and you, too, our kids'll look just as good as any of the other groups. You'll like DeWitt, Shanny. I imagine you have a lot in common with him, what with the music and all."

I wondered how the conversation got centered on DeWitt when I was aiming toward Thor. I wanted to flap my arms at Aunt Adabelle and yell "Hah! Hah!"— the way Thor had done at Blastoff to get him headed in the right direction.

"Thor seemed really excited about the drums," I said, steering us back the way I wanted to go. "And Twyla did, too."

"Well, sure. With DeWitt sounding like a whole orchestra with that gadget of his and then you with the drums, we'll have the best music in the whole competition." Aunt Adabelle lifted the spoon she was stirring with and tasted the soup, then added a sprinkle of something from a jar on a little shelf above the stove. "DeWitt's a real interesting boy. Lots of talent."

It sounded like the old bait-and-switch game to me. Aunt Adabelle had baited me here with Thor and his Sex Appeal, and she was now switching me to DeWitt and his talent. Who wants to trade Sex Appeal for talent? I didn't even get to ask what kind of gadget it was that DeWitt had all this talent with because Bucky came in just then.

"You've missed just about all of 'All My Children,' " he said, looking at Aunt Adabelle.

"Bucky comes over every day to watch that soap opera with me," Aunt Adabelle explained. "Well, Bucky, I just wanted to fix a nice dinner for Shanny so she wouldn't pack right up and go home again."

Bucky looked at me, worried. "You're not going to do that, are you?" he asked. "I've been waiting all morning for you to get up. I went upstairs about five times to see if you were awake yet."

"My lands, Bucky," Aunt Adabelle said. "Not everyone gets up with the chickens. Shanny had a long trip yesterday. Likely she'll get up earlier tomorrow." Hoisting the pot of soup from the stove to the table, she motioned for me and Bucky to sit down. Evidently it wasn't unusual for Bucky to eat there.

Bucky hesitated, looking suspiciously at the pot. "What is it?"

"Suicide Soup," Aunt Adabelle said. "And cornbread.

With new lettuce and radishes from the garden for a salad and fresh strawberries for dessert."

Bucky sat down. "Some days it's not worth staying for," he confided.

Aunt Adabelle didn't seem to mind. "Some days I don't care to stay myself. But this is my specialty. It was always a big favorite with your mom and The Cousins, Shanny." She ladled the soup into three bowls.

I picked up my spoon and stirred around in my bowl. "What's in it?" I lean toward Big Macs and french fries.

"Be adventurous," Aunt Adabelle said. "Just eat."

I ate. It was delicious.

From the living room I could hear the closing music for "All My Children."

"Thor said," I began, getting back to the subject I was trying to research, "that there isn't anybody else in town who plays the drums."

"Oh, I forgot." Bucky put down the spoon he had been slurping from. "Thor and Twyla are going to Pratt. Thor told me to tell you he won't be over today."

Bucky said "Thor and Twyla" as if they belonged together—like salt and pepper or bacon and eggs.

Well, there was always DeWitt for me, or Bucky. After all, when I was thirty, Bucky would be twenty-three.

I wished I had stayed in Los Angeles.

"You know what we're going to do today?" Bucky asked as we cleaned up the dinner dishes. "I'm going to show you the ranch." Evidently he considered me to be his summer playmate. I hoped he wasn't anything like Flame's little brother. We were always trying to get rid of him, and he was always trying to stay with us.

27

"I'm supposed to be here to help Aunt Adabelle get ready to move," I told him. "I imagine she has things for me to do."

"Well, there's no hurry about that," Aunt Adabelle said so sharply that I glanced at her. I couldn't read anything in her face, though, and she went on. "You go on and have a look around. There's plenty of time to think about packing up."

Bucky took hold of my hand as if I were a little kid who needed to be led around. "First we'll go out and say hello to old Blastoff. After that I'll show you the creek and the pasture where the yellow roses grow; then we'll go on up to the Bride's House."

"Oh, say, if you're going up to the Bride's House, I'll walk up there with you." Aunt Adabelle went to the refrigerator and started pulling stuff out of it. "I'll pack up some dinner to take for Shirley while you go out to the corral, and I'll meet you there."

I hadn't known anybody lived in the Bride's House. But there were a whole lot of things I didn't know about the ranch. Most of it I wasn't too eager to learn about, either.

Bucky tugged at my hand. "Let's go. Blastoff will be anxious to see us."

If Blastoff was anxious about anything, it didn't show. He was kind of leaning against the corral rails when we got there. His eyes were closed, and if it hadn't been for his tail, which switched listlessly at a fly, I would have said he had passed away standing up.

"Hey, Blastoff," Bucky yelled.

The horse didn't move. Bucky turned to me. "He's pretty deaf." He pronounced it "deef."

Letting go of my hand, Bucky crawled up on the corral rail alongside Blastoff and stroked his skinny neck. "Hey," he yelled, "it's time to get up." He jumped back down to the ground.

Blastoff's ears flicked forward, and he opened his eyes. He looked at Bucky and nickered softly, deep in his chest, then peered at me. Suddenly he came to life. Heaving himself away from the railing, he tossed his head up and down a couple of times. His big upper lip lifted in the sneer he had shown me yesterday, and he began a stiff little dance around the corral.

"He loves to show off when there's someone to see him," Bucky said. "He used to be the meanest bucking bronco in the whole state of Idaho."

"I heard him running around the corral in the night," I said.

Bucky nodded. "Yeah. His eyes aren't so good. He thinks the shadows are people, so he puts on a whole show on moonlight nights."

I looked at Blastoff. His ears were laid back, and his head was down. As I watched, he went into a creaky spin, then lifted his back hooves off the ground in a vicious buck, snorting and grunting with the effort.

Bucky watched him proudly. "I'm going to ride him in the Pioneer Day rodeo. I've been practicing."

I was alarmed. "My gosh, Bucky, isn't he dangerous?"

"Yeah," Bucky said. "But they don't let him go on rodeo tours anymore, and that makes him feel bad. So I'm going to ride him and show him he's still the greatest horse around."

"Does Aunt Adabelle know you ride him?" I asked, watching the old nag buck stiffly all around the corral.

"We-e-ell." Bucky traced a furrow in the dirt with the toe of his shoe. "Like yesterday I was going to curry him, and I left both the corral gate and the barn door open when I went to get the curry comb. Blastoff snuck out of the corral and into the barn and started eating the stuff Aunt Adabelle gives her chickens, and I couldn't get him out, so she had to come and chase him. So she knows I'm here a lot."

He hadn't exactly answered my question. I wondered if I ought to snitch on him, but Thor had said something to Bucky the day before about messing around with the old horse. Maybe I should just stay out of it.

As if thinking about him made him materialize, Thor drove into the yard in his blue truck with the thunderbolt—Twyla's thunderbolt—painted on its door.

My heart beat a drum roll. Bucky had said that Thor wasn't coming, but here he was. He had dumped Twyla and come to see me! Or maybe he had decided he'd rather have *me* go with him to Pratt than Twyla.

"Hi, Shanny," he said as he stopped the truck and got out. "How's everything going today?"

"Bucky was just giving me the grand tour of the ranch," I said, then wished I hadn't because maybe Thor would think I'd rather do that than go with him.

"Bucky's the right guy to do it." Thor came over and ruffled Bucky's hair. "He knows every inch of the territory."

Bucky smiled with shy pride. "I thought you and Twyla were going to Pratt."

Thor nodded. "We are. I'm on my way to pick up Twyla right now. I just stopped by here to get Aunt Adabelle's shopping list." He headed for the house.

Salt and pepper. Bacon and eggs. Twyla and Thor.

"I guess Thor really likes Twyla, doesn't he?" I blurted, then felt ashamed for trying to pump information from a little kid like Bucky.

"I guess so." Bucky looked up at me. "But *I* like *you* better, Shanny." He pulled a withered apple from his pocket. "I brought this for Blastoff, but you can have it if you want it."

I took it from his outstretched hand. It was sticky and covered with lint from his pocket.

Thor came out of the house just then and got into his truck. Leaning out of the window, he said, "Don't you have a 'Did you know' for me today, Shanny?"

"Sure." I walked closer to the truck. "Did you know there was a lady in South Africa who made a will leaving all her money to her seven pet lizards when she died?"

"That's a good one, Shanny." Thor started his truck, waved, and drove away.

While I watched him go, Aunt Adabelle came out carrying a paper bag in her hand, which I assumed held Shirley's dinner.

Looking at the apple in my hand, I said, "I'm not very hungry right now. Maybe Shirley would like to have this with her dinner."

Bucky giggled as he took the apple. "Shirley doesn't eat anything like that." He took my hand again, and the three of us started up the hill to the Bride's House. The road was narrow and rocky, and I was sort of glad that Bucky was holding my hand and steering me around the bigger rocks. I wondered if Aunt Adabelle might need help, but she seemed well acquainted with the path.

From down below, the Bride's House looked run-

31

down, but up close it seemed kind of snug and cozy. The windows sparkled as if they had just been washed, and pretty flowered curtains showed through them.

"It looks as if Shirley takes real good care of the Bride's House," I said.

Aunt Adabelle laughed. "Shirley lives under the back porch. Bucky, you take Shanny around there and see if you can coax Shirley to come out while I talk with Uncle Vic." She handed him the paper bag and went on into the Bride's House.

I stood staring after her. She had said the whole thing in such a normal tone that it took me a moment to really *hear* the words. What did she mean, ". . . talk with Uncle Vic"?

Numbly I followed Bucky around the side of the little house where the mystery of Shirley under the back porch was cleared up. Shirley was a skinny, bedraggled black-and-white cat who peered suspiciously from her lair.

"She's still pretty scared." Bucky squatted down and held out a bit of meat, which he took from the paper bag. "She just came a couple of weeks ago, and me'n Aunt Adabelle have been taking care of her. We named her Shirley because she's not very pretty, and we thought it would be nice to give her a fancy name to make her feel better."

I wasn't really listening to him. I was tuned in to the faint murmur of Aunt Adabelle's voice inside the house.

"Bucky," I said, "who lives here?"

"Nobody." Bucky held the piece of food very still as Shirley crept forward to sniff it.

"Aunt Adabelle's talking to somebody," I said. "Did she say she was going to talk with Uncle Vic?"

32

Shirley grabbed the food and slunk back under the porch. Bucky looked up. "That's what she said. She visits with him almost every day." He dug into the bag for more food.

Inside the house, Aunt Adabelle laughed as if someone had said something funny.

"Bucky," I said, "Uncle Vic is *dead*."

Bucky's eyes opened wide as if he had never thought of that before.

"Here," he said, standing up and shoving the bag of food at me. "You feed Shirley. I'm going home."

Totally bewildered, I watched him go. This was going to be quite a summer, what with a neurotic cat who hid under a porch, an old horse who saw phantoms in the night, and an elderly aunt who talked with a dead man.

4

I couldn't help wondering if Mom and The Cousins might have good reason for wanting to put Aunt Adabelle in a retirement home. I mean, if she went around talking to dead people, wasn't that reason enough? But if they knew about it, why hadn't they warned me? Maybe they thought I wouldn't have come if I had known, which was true.

But if they *didn't* know about the way she was, then what? Should I tell?

I sighed. Those sunny beaches of California seemed like another world, one from which I had been banished. I wondered if I would ever get back to that lazy, carefree life.

Well, first things first. I would have to decide what to do about Aunt Adabelle later. Right now Shirley looked as if she might cave in if she didn't get some food inside her.

Kneeling down, I held out a chunk of meat that looked

as if it might have been fished out of Aunt Adabelle's Suicide Soup. "Here, Shirley," I coaxed.

The cat backed away from me.

"Here, dummy," I said, poking the meat at her.

She hissed and ran back under the porch. I could see her eyes shining in the murky dimness there.

I wheedled and coaxed and even lay down and reached my hand in to put the food right in front of her, but all Shirley did was whack my hand and snarl. I couldn't help admiring her courage for attacking someone so much bigger than she was.

"Just leave the food there on the ground," Aunt Adabelle said. "She'll get it after we leave."

I bumped my head as I hauled myself out from under the porch. Aunt Adabelle had come out so silently that I wondered if she had floated right through the wall or something. My mouth fell open as I stared up at her, but I couldn't think of any words to put into it, so I closed it again.

"She's not friendly, poor thing," Aunt Adabelle said. "Doesn't trust anybody yet."

I found my voice. "But if she's so hungry, why won't she eat?"

"She has her reasons." Aunt Adabelle looked around. "What's happened to Bucky?"

I put the food down and stood up. "He went on home."

Aunt Adabelle looked puzzled. "He doesn't usually do that. Why did he leave?"

I couldn't think how to tell her why Bucky had been so spooked, so I just worked up a grin and said, "He had his reasons."

35

For the rest of the day I wondered if I ought to say something to Aunt Adabelle about how it was pretty weird the way she talked with Uncle Vic up there at the Bride's House. But how do you start up a conversation like that? Do you casually slide into it, like, "Oh, say, by the way, Aunt Adabelle, did you know Uncle Vic checked out nearly four years ago?" Or should I hit her with something like, "If you don't clean up your act, you'll land in something worse than a retirement home"?

There was just no way to get into it. Maybe she actually thought she saw Uncle Vic there in the Bride's House. What did I know about psychology? I've had Mr. Sutro's class, but a year of high school psych doesn't exactly qualify a person to be a therapist.

Besides, there didn't seem to be anything wrong with Aunt Adabelle other than that. I mean, compared to what wanders the streets back home, she was a textbook of normal behavior. Her memory was certainly A-OK. After we returned from the Bride's House, she told me a lot of stuff about when my mom and The Cousins stayed with her. She remembered all kinds of little details, such as the way Mom fixed her hair and the guys she went out with.

It was hard for me to think of my mom as a girl like me. Well, in the first place she never was a girl like me. I mean, my mom is the kind who inspires confidence. She's an investment counselor, and people ask her for advice—even pay for it. Nobody has ever asked me for my advice, except Flame, who asked once if she should wear purple eyeshadow or green with her new silver Liberace cloak that we found in our favorite thrift shop.

"I believe your mother and The Cousins left some

scrapbooks here that you might like to look at," Aunt Adabelle said.

It might be kind of fun to look at something like that. "Maybe we'll run across them when we start packing your stuff."

"Oh, pshaw, Shanny, I told you before not to worry about that. Just take time to find out what's going on around here."

Maybe that was a good opening to bring up what was going on with her up at the Bride's House. But I still couldn't figure out how to say it, so instead I blurted out, "Speaking of what's going on, I was just wondering if you maybe know whether or not Thor and Twyla are, you know, sort of semi-engaged or anything like that."

Aunt Adabelle smiled. "What you want to know is whether Thor is still running loose so that you can have a whirl at lassoing him."

I grinned sheepishly.

"He would have told me if he was fenced in," Aunt Adabelle said. "Far as I know, he and Twyla are just good friends."

I wondered if he really would have told her if he and Twyla were more than just friends. Didn't seventeen-year-old guys keep some things to themselves?

Even so, the whole summer had changed colors. Up until then it had seemed mostly kind of drab gray, but Aunt Adabelle's words painted it bright yellow. I could handle anything if Thor was dangling like a carrot up ahead of me.

"He'll be coming over to clean out my henhouse to-morrow," Aunt Adabelle said. "Maybe he could use some help."

The glamour of the California beaches faded. Aunt Adabelle's henhouse was Where It Was At.

I forgot all about tattling on Bucky and the way he was messing around with Blastoff. The next morning I was in my room experimenting with some new mousse hairstyling gel stuff when I happened to look out of the window and saw Bucky heading for the corral. Turning back to the mirror, I spiked a few more clumps of hair and asked myself if it was really any of my business what he did. Thor knew about it, didn't he? He had said something about it to Bucky the first day I came. I didn't want to get involved. Besides, I wanted time to fix myself up before Thor came to clean the henhouse so that he couldn't fail to notice how different I was. He had liked me "different" that first day. When something works, why change it?

Bucky was climbing the rails of the corral fence when I looked out again, but he just perched there and looked at Blastoff, who was standing with his head at half mast. Blastoff didn't exactly look dangerous. Maybe I would just wait to see if Bucky tried to ride him, and if Blastoff went berserk, I would rush out and save him just as Thor arrived so he would be impressed again at how good I was at handling horses.

But then the old horse came to life, tossing his head and pawing at the dirt with one hoof.

Sighing, I put down my comb, knowing it was my duty to do what I could to make sure Bucky didn't get hurt. Even the *old* Shanny would do that, and surely this new one I was supposed to discover there on the ranch would, too.

Yanking on my army fatigue pants and my favorite

black T-shirt with the picture of Boy George on the front, I ran downstairs. I stopped on the last step when I heard an unfamiliar voice coming from the kitchen. In the background, the introductory music for "All My Children" was playing, and I wondered why Bucky didn't come in to watch.

"Lardy," the unfamiliar voice was saying, "I can't even read a newspaper anymore without there be a new story about them city people hacking one another up. You sure that girl you took in is all right?"

"Of course she's all right." Aunt Adabelle sounded huffy. "She's a sweet girl, and I enjoy having her here."

"Well, *I* heard she's a real strange one," the other woman said.

"Oh?" Aunt Adabelle's voice went up in a question. "And where did you hear a thing like that, Perlie?"

"Well, *lardy*, Adabelle. Fern Timmons was right *there* when the bus come in, and that shameless girl bounced off and grabbed Mona Horspool's boy in broad daylight." Perlie punctuated her words with a couple of thumps on the table. "And them *clothes*. Her dad *must* could afford something better than them *rags*, even if he *is* just a pickle. *Lardy!*"

"Fern Timmons gave you a rundown on her clothes, too, did she?" Aunt Adabelle said.

I didn't want to hear all this, so I turned to go back upstairs. But a stair creaked, and Aunt Adabelle must have heard it because she called, "Shanny? Shanny, would you come in here?"

I wished I hadn't been playing around with that hairstyling mousse because I looked pretty weird, and I didn't want to embarrass Aunt Adabelle. But she yelled out

39

again for me to come, so what could I do? She blinked when I walked into the kitchen, where she and Perlie sat at the table, but then she went on as smooth as if she were introducing the Queen of England.

"Perlie," she said, "I'd like you to meet my grandniece, Shannon Alder. Shanny, this is Perlie Truesdale."

Perlie was a big lady whose bosom made her look as if she were sitting in a pile of pillows.

Sorting through my mental computer, I located some manners my mom had taught me when I was a little kid. Walking up to Perlie Truesdale, I offered my hand and said, "I'm very happy to meet you."

Perlie leaned away from me. "Likewise, I'm sure." Her eyes toured my frame, ending up with my spiked hair. "Lardy," she whispered.

Hoisting herself from her chair, she hurried toward the door. "I better be getting along," she said. "Melvin'll be wondering what's happened to me."

"Come again," Aunt Adabelle said politely as she stood up and followed Perlie to the door.

"I'll do that." Perlie stepped carefully down the steps of the front porch. "Lardy," we heard her mutter as she churned toward her car.

Aunt Adabelle watched her go. "She can hardly wait to get on the party line. She can stir up more dirt with the telephone than with a broom." She sighed. "Shanny, I'm afraid she's going to spread things around so that folks will be a mite standoffish until they get to know the real you."

"Lardy!" I said, and we both collapsed on kitchen chairs and laughed until we were weak.

Aunt Adabelle knew all about the way Bucky was trying to ride old Blastoff.

"Oh, sure," she said after I told her about what I knew. "He's been sneaking around riding that old horse all summer. Frustrates the tar out of him when he gets on Blastoff and the old plug won't buck."

"But isn't he dangerous?" I sputtered. "I mean, I've seen Blastoff in action with my own eyes. Don't you think Bucky is going to get hurt?"

"Not by Blastoff. He's too old to be dangerous. Besides, he adores Bucky. Whenever Bucky gets on him, he walks around as if he's stepping on eggs. He knows Bucky's too little to be his old enemy, the cowboy. But that's what makes Bucky so mad."

"But . . . but . . . but . . ." I sounded like a motorboat. "But Thor said Blastoff is dangerous. And what about the day I came? Blastoff was about to stomp my drums. And how about the way he bucks all around the corral?"

"Well, honey, he might have bumbled into those drums because he couldn't see them. He's close to being blind, you know. But he wouldn't hurt anybody on purpose. And those shows he puts on in the corral—that's all they are, just shows. He likes to remember the days when people cheered him for acting mean."

Then what was the big deal about my being so gutsy? I could feel my heart begin to slide down toward my toes. "But on the day I came, Thor told Bucky he should stay away from Blastoff or he'd likely get mangled."

"It's all pretend." Aunt Adabelle went to the refrigerator and stooped over to pull out some leftovers for our noon dinner. "See, Thor and I decided both Bucky and Blastoff could use a little boost in the self-esteem

41

department. You can't help but feel sorry for that old horse. And Bucky, he spends a lot of time alone. So we let both of them think that we believe Blastoff is still dangerous. It makes both of them feel as if they're really something." She stood up and carried a couple of bowls to the counter and emptied them into some pans.

I watched, my heart crashing in flames. The old horse was harmless, which meant that Thor was making fun of me when he made out that I was so heroic. I could imagine him laughing with Twyla about it, his lip lifting in a sneer like Blastoff's. What a moron I had been, thinking he *liked* me, for cripes' sake. How pathetic can you be? That carrot that was dangling up ahead of me had just turned into a turnip.

I was down by the corral watching Bucky curry Blastoff when Thor came to clean the henhouse. The first thing he said was, "Hi, Shanny. Had your daily adventure with Blastoff yet?"

"Not yet," I said. "I thought maybe I'd do something really dangerous today, like go have a fist fight with a kitten."

Thor looked surprised, then embarrassed.

"I know how dangerous Blastoff is," I continued. "There's not much to be proud of for slapping a half blind old horse like him. But I guess you thought I looked so freaky it was all right to make fun of me."

"Oh, gosh, Shanny, I'm sorry," Thor said. "It wasn't because you looked freaky. I mean, you didn't look freaky. But I guess I did do a snow job on you. But look, you didn't *know* Blastoff was harmless. So I still think it took a lot of courage to do what you did."

Still seething, I thought about that. Maybe he was right. Maybe courage comes from standing up to what you *think* is dangerous, like Shirley hissing at me when all I wanted to do was feed her. That sounded like something to write to my folks so they could congratulate themselves on how smart they were to send me to the ranch.

"I apologize, Shanny." Thor held out his hand. "Still friends?"

I hesitated, then grasped his hand. It made my arm tingle clear up to my ears. "Okay. Still friends. I'll even help you clean out the henhouse to show I don't hold any grudges."

Thor grinned. "Offer accepted. But first come on over to my truck. I brought the road-show music for you to look at. Don't forget, I'll be coming by tomorrow to pick up you and your drums."

My drums. Had he given me a snow job about my drums, too? About how much they needed me? Would I go there on Saturday morning and find that they could do just fine with DeWitt and his gadget and all his talent, and they didn't need me at all and would just roll their eyes like Perlie Truesdale and snicker behind their hands?

The summer was taking on a drab gray tinge again. Lardy!

5

The less said about the henhouse the better. I learned that hens aren't housebroken, so the straw covering their floor was pretty mucky, which was, of course, why Thor was cleaning it out. I wished I hadn't offered to help. In fact, if it hadn't been for Bucky, I would have told Thor I had an urgent letter to write, or something else noble like that, and gone back to the house. But when Bucky, who came to give a hand, too, looked at me admiringly and said, "I'm glad you don't barf like Twyla did when she was helping us," I knew I'd stay if it killed me.

I made like it was no big deal and said, "Oh, I've done worse jobs than this," although I couldn't think of any.

Bucky didn't mention anything about what had happened at the Bride's House the day before, so I didn't either. I wanted to talk it over with Thor before I stirred up a lot of trouble by writing to Mom and The Cousins.

But the henhouse didn't seem like exactly the right place to bring it up.

Aunt Adabelle had about a hundred hens, and as we worked, they all talked at once, clucking with interest and scratching at the smelly litter we raked out. I decided I wasn't ever going to eat any more eggs—not after seeing where they came from.

Thor was very cheerful. I guess he was used to working in that muck. He made up silly songs for Bucky, such as:

"There was an old speckled cluck,
Who belonged to a nice kid named Buck.
She laid colored eggs
As big as beer kegs.
That cluck brought our Buck lots of luck."

Bucky giggled and asked me to make up a song. I said I didn't know how but that I would beat out a rhythm while Thor sang that one. So I got a couple of sticks and whacked out a beat while Thor sang.

It was a lot of fun. But after we brought in new straw for the chickens, Thor left, probably for a date with Just-Friends Twyla.

When he thanked me for helping with the henhouse, he said, "Shanny, you were super. Not many girls would get out and work like that."

I didn't think he was snowing me this time. And I would have my chance to be alone with him the next day when he came to get me and my drums for the rehearsal. That made me happy.

Just in case we should run out of conversation, I stocked up on Esoteric Facts that night. I wondered if Thor knew it took only sixty days for a housefly to become a great-grandmother. Or that Henry Ford forgot to put a reverse gear in his first automobile.

The next morning after breakfast I searched through my duffel bag for something on the quiet side to wear. If Perlie Truesdale had been broadcasting the way Aunt Adabelle thought she would, the people at the rehearsal would be expecting something really far out. So why not surprise them and show up looking as normal as Twyla?

But no matter how many times I stirred through my duffel bag, I couldn't come up with any Twyla-type shorts and T-shirts.

Flame would have said, "If you've got the name, you might as well play the game." So I put on my Boy George outfit and hauled my drums downstairs.

I was ready an hour early, not that I was eager or anything. To pass the time, I went back upstairs and pulled a notebook from my duffel bag. Mom had made me bring it, saying I ought to keep a journal while I was there. I guess she thought I would want a record of the miracles that were going to happen to Shape Up Shanny.

At the top of a page I wrote: "Things I've Learned about Myself." Underneath, I wrote:

1. I'm not afraid of horses (as long as they are old and half blind).
2. I don't barf in henhouses.

They weren't exactly prime qualifications for the job of President of the United States, but you have to begin somewhere.

"DeWitt didn't get back from Pocatello," Thor said as he loaded up my drums. "We'll have to get along with Loydene on the piano. But maybe you can see what we'll be doing."

Thor whistled cheerily as we got into the truck, and he started the engine. He was happy, and I hoped a little of it had to do with being with me.

"That's some of the music from the show," he said when he came to the end of a tune.

I didn't recognize it. "Thor, just exactly what is a road show? This is all new to me." I settled happily into my seat in the truck, wishing that the rehearsal was in Montana or somewhere like that so we'd be alone together for a long time.

"Okay, I'll explain." Thor drove out onto the highway, past the calligraphy-decorated mailbox—a little reminder of Twyla. "They won't exactly be *road* shows this year since we're not traveling. We usually put the shows on in three different places the same night, so we're on the road. But this year we're having this big Pioneer Day bash, and everybody decided to have all the shows here that night as part of the celebration." He stopped, and his forehead wrinkled up as if he were worried. "I sure hope ours goes okay. We're having some real problems with it."

"I'm still not exactly sure what a road show *is*," I said. "Evidently you can do away with the road part, but what about the *show*? Who shows what?"

Thor laughed, the deep sound of it vibrating in my ears, making my heart jog a little faster. I mean, I could have done a whole course of aerobics just sitting there in the cab with Thor.

"Road show," Thor said, grinning at me. "In Thor's Dictionary of Unfamiliar Terms, we find this definition."

I waited for him to go on, but he was looking in the rear-view mirror, back toward Aunt Adabelle's place.

"I wonder why Aunt Adabelle is going up to the Bride's House at this time of day," he said. "She always says it takes her most of the day to get into gear to make it up the hill."

I looked back and saw Aunt Adabelle trudging toward the Bride's House. She didn't carry anything this time, like the brown paper bag with Shirley's dinner in it.

"I don't think she's going up to feed Shirley," I said. "I guess you know all about Shirley."

Thor nodded. "I remember the day somebody dumped Shirley off. They probably knew Aunt Adabelle takes in strays. She's going to have kittens, you know. Shirley, I mean, not Aunt Adabelle."

"I didn't know about the kittens. Maybe Aunt Adabelle's going up there to help her have them."

"Oh, it's not time for that yet." Thor peered into the rear-view mirror again, and I turned, but we had gone around a curve and couldn't see Aunt Adabelle anymore.

Thor speeded up. "We can find out when we get back home."

I cleared my throat. "Thor, did you know that Aunt Adabelle talks to Uncle Vic there in the Bride's House?"

He glanced over at me, his mouth curving a little as if he were waiting for the punch line to a joke. "Okay, I'll bite. What does she talk to him about?"

"Thor, I'm serious. She *talks* to him—or with him.

She talks and laughs, and she waits in between as if she's listening for him to say something. It's as if she were talking on the telephone or something."

Thor turned his eyes back to the road. "Does Bucky know about this?"

"Yes. I guess he's been up there with her a lot when she's been talking to Uncle Vic. But evidently he didn't think about it being kind of weird until day before yesterday when *I* got spooked about it."

Thor nodded slowly. "That's why he hasn't been too anxious to go over to Aunt Adabelle's the past couple of days, except to take care of Blastoff. Mom thought he was sick. She's been taking his temperature and feeding him yogurt."

The mention of Thor's mom surprised me. I hadn't really thought of him as having a mom like everybody else. It was like you never think of a teacher as having any kind of life except the part that affects you.

I wondered if his mom was like mine, always prodding him to improve his life. But I didn't think Thor's life needed much improving. He seemed to have it all together. He *knew* who he was.

I brought my mind back to Aunt Adabelle. "I just wondered if you knew about it."

"I didn't," Thor said. "She keeps the Bride's House just the way it was when she and Uncle Vic lived there. You know—rag rugs, kerosene lamps, old-fashioned wood-burning stove, and all that. But I didn't know she thought *he* was there, too."

He rubbed the side of his face with one hand, and it rasped a little as if he needed a shave. I had never been out with a guy who actually grew *whiskers*, and I wanted

49

to reach over and rub his cheek myself. I wondered how it would feel against my own cheek.

"I don't think she's very thrilled about going to a retirement home," I said. "Do you think that would make her weird?"

Thor considered it. "Maybe. Or maybe it's because she's alone so much and just talks to people who aren't there so she'll have someone to talk to. I'm glad you're there with her now, Shanny."

"My folks thought I'd enjoy being here with her," I said, deciding not to go into anything like the Great Dog-Food Caper with Thor. "Mom and The Cousins spent several summers here when they were young."

Thor turned onto a little road that led up a hill. "Aunt Adabelle never had any children, even though she and Uncle Vic built that big house so they could have a whole bunch. When they didn't get any, they sort of adopted everybody else's kids. I guess any young person in Wolf Creek would be glad to live there with Aunt Adabelle the way you're doing." Driving into a paved parking lot in front of a red-brick church, he stopped the truck. "Well, here we are in beautiful downtown Wolf Creek," he said.

I looked around. "Downtown" to me meant tall buildings, or at least a Winchell's Donut Shop and some Golden Arches. But all I could see here besides the church were a couple of houses and another red-brick building that said "Wolf Creek School" on a sign above the door. There were half a dozen cows chewing grass in front of the schoolhouse, and I could see a cemetery behind the church.

"This is the town?" I asked.

Thor grinned. "We used to have a general store over there west of the school, but it's gone. The school is closed because we bus everybody to Pratt now. Even the blacksmith shop is closed since the blacksmith moved away. The only thing that's still in use is the church, which is where we're going to rehearse."

"The church and the *cemetery*," I said. "That's still in use, too, isn't it?" I was going to make some smart remark about what a dead place Wolf Creek was, but I decided Thor might not appreciate it.

Thor looked up the hill to the green lawns of the cemetery. "Yes, it's still in use. There are some really great people up there, like Uncle Vic." His gaze shifted to the mountains that surrounded the valley. "You know, Shanny, I really love this place. I'm going to miss it when I go away to college."

I was glad I hadn't made the rude remark about the town being dead because I think that probably would have cooled things with Thor. I didn't want to do that, not now that things were going so well.

I could see about a dozen kids on the steps of the church, and more were arriving. A VW came churning into the parking lot with a carroty-haired girl sticking up out of the sun roof.

"Hey, Thor," she yelled, "what's happening, man?" Although she spoke to Thor, she stared at me.

Thor waved back. "That's Loydene," he told me as we got out of the truck. "She's the one who's going to play the piano today." He didn't sound any too happy about it.

Another girl came up as we unloaded my drums. "My allergies are in full bloob," she said. "I'b not goig to be

51

able to sig today." Honking her nose in a tissue, she looked at me. "I'b Berda Wigger," she told me.

"Hi," I said. "I'm Shanny Alder."

Berda nodded. "I was thiggig that's who you had to be." She eyed my hair and my clothes.

Thor put a hand on her arm. "We'll work around you today, but do you think you'll be okay by Pioneer Day? Or should we get somebody else to do your solo?"

"I'll be fide by thed," Berda said. "I really wadt to do the part."

A big guy came over and began gathering up my drums. "Call me U Haul," he said with a grin. "I'm the official carryall."

They all seemed friendly enough, but I noticed that their eyes skidded away when they looked at me. Two girls on the lawn whispered behind their hands. Others kind of sidled away as Thor and I followed U Haul and my drums across the parking lot.

On the lawn several guys were hammering boards together.

"The scenery committee," Thor said. "Twyla designed all of our sets. She and I went to Pratt and got all the lumber on Thursday. Look how much they've already got done."

All I could see was that they had nailed together something that looked like several open closets, with shelves and spaces. The main thing I was interested in was what Thor had said. He and Twyla had gone to Pratt to get lumber. So that's what the trip had been about. It wasn't like a date at all. Maybe Aunt Adabelle was right. Maybe they were just good friends.

Thor took me inside the church to what he called the

cultural hall, where I saw people everywhere. Several women crawled around on the floor, cutting bolts of cloth. Costume committee, Thor said. Some guys were tossing a basketball around, which seemed to have nothing to do with the show. A group of girls was going through a tap routine over in one corner, and I saw that Loydene was one of them. A dark-haired girl ran around with a clipboard, saying something to all the girls.

The whole busy scene reminded me of Aunt Adabelle's henhouse.

I could see right away that I wasn't going to fit in. Everybody else looked as if they had come to be in "Little House on the Prairie." I belonged in "Tuff Turf."

The girl with the clipboard dashed over as I was setting up my drums.

"Hi," she said. "I'm Dot Myers." She looked me over the way some of the other people had done, and I thought she wasn't going to say any more. But then she went on. "I'm taking the names of all the girls who are going to try out for Pioneer Day Queen. Are you going to?"

"I don't think so," I said.

Dot looked relieved. "Let me know if you change your mind."

"Okay." I wasn't really paying much attention because I was watching Twyla, who had just spotted Thor. Running over to him, she pushed up so close that he was practically wearing her. If they were just good friends, nobody had bothered to tell her. I tried to hear what she was saying to him, but they were too far away.

Then Twyla put a couple of fingers in her mouth and blew a shrill whistle that got everyone's attention. That girl had endless talents.

Thor jumped up on the stage. "All right, you guys," he yelled. "Let's get going or we'll be here all day."

He seemed to be in charge. He introduced me and told them that I would be playing the drums for the show. There were a few murmurs around the hall, but I couldn't hear the words.

Loydene came running over and plumped herself down on the piano bench. "Oh, lardy," she said, "I wish DeWitt would get back. I can't play the piano worth a fig."

Lardy?

"Are you related to Perlie Truesdale?" I asked.

"Lardy, yes. She's my grandmother." Loydene looked surprised. "How did you know?"

"Just a lucky guess," I said.

"I know something about you," Loydene said. "Your dad's on TV." I could tell she was impressed. "Hey, you guys," she yelled at a bunch of girls who were going up on the stage, "did you know Shanny's dad's on TV?"

"Really?" one of them said. They looked at me with a little more interest than before.

"He's just a pickle," I said modestly. "You know, in the pickle commercial."

"Lardy," Loydene said, "I'd be a *wart* on a pickle if I could just be on TV."

"I've seen him," one girl said. "Is that really your dad?"

"Come on, come on," Thor yelled. "You girls in the chorus line take your places. Where's Bill Jacobson?"

"He can't be here today," somebody said.

Thor groaned. "This thing is coming off in two weeks, and nobody comes to rehearsals. No wonder it's not going very well."

"Thor," Loydene called, "did you know Shanny's dad is on TV?"

The people who hadn't heard it before looked over at me now. Their faces showed interest. I felt important. I had never gotten that kind of attention at home because there were a lot of kids in my school whose dads were on TV or in the movies.

"Yes, I did know," Thor said. "She'll be able to help us a lot. She can tell us what we're doing wrong." He clapped his hands for attention, not waiting for Twyla's whistle this time. "Before we get started, we'll have Shanny give us one of her facts. She knows more of them than a set of encyclopedias." He bowed toward me as if he were introducing some big, important person.

I felt put on the spot, but I remembered a fact that seemed appropriate. "Did you know," I said, "that the No. 1 worst fear of human beings is speaking before a group?"

"I believe it!" U Haul said, and several people laughed. I was grateful to Thor because I felt I had picked up a few points, and I think I picked up a few more when I began beating my drums.

The show was entitled "As Is," and that's about all I could figure out about it. There was a lot of giggling and messing around, and I couldn't tell what was in the script and what was just goofing off. The girls who did the tap routine were good, though, and I could tell there were some nice voices when they all sang.

Loydene thumped her way through the music somehow. I hadn't heard any of it before, but I tried to keep up. I wasn't very impressed with any of it, at least the way Loydene played it.

The show dragged, and the only good thing about it was that it was short. When we had gone all the way through it, everybody looked at me—the daughter of the TV personality, the one who knew all about show business.

"Well," Thor said, "what do you think of it?"

They expected me to know a lot about it, so why not take my dad's advice and act the part? Besides, Thor had been talking about how something was wrong with it.

"You've got a lot going for you," I said to soften the blow, "but the show is a real bomb. Couldn't you find one with a better script?"

The sudden quiet would have done justice to the cemetery behind the church. I looked around, puzzled. People were looking from me to Thor and then back at me. Thor stood as if he'd been shot but hadn't yet gotten around to falling over.

"Lardy," Loydene whispered, "you really blew it. Didn't you know that Thor *wrote* the show?"

6

Talk about blowing it. I couldn't have done a better job if I'd been a typhoon. The weather there in the big hall changed from warm and clearing to a complete freeze-out. I was alone again, as if I were in one of those little isolation booths they use on TV game shows, all glassed in away from everyone else.

Kids began to turn their backs to me, whispering behind their hands. One girl spoke loud enough for me to hear. "Well," she said, "what do you *expect* from a second-generation pickle?"

Twyla was moving toward Thor as if to protect him. I thought she was going to launch a warhead of words at me, but instead she said gently, "Shanny didn't mean that the way it sounded, did you, Shanny?"

"I was just going to say that myself." I scrambled out from my nest of drums, trying to think of some kind of tourniquet that would stop the flow of Thor's bleeding confidence. "What I *meant* was, it was the *run-through* that wasn't so good. It was the first time through today, and we weren't warmed up yet."

"And a lot of people aren't here to do their parts," Twyla put in.

"And Berda Wigger couldn't sing with her sinuses stuffed up," I said.

"That's *Merna Winger*," Loydene whispered.

Oh, boy! I was getting in deeper. But how was I to know? That's the way *she* had said her name.

Thor put up a hand. "Look, it's all right. I asked for an honest opinion, and I got it. After all, I'm not exactly Rodgers and Hammerstein. The show *is* a bomb. That's why it hasn't been going so well."

"No, Thor, listen." I swam through a sea of hostility to stand in front of him. "Thor, my mouth is like a 7-Eleven store—open day and night. I should rent it out as a flycatcher. What do I know about what makes a show good or bad?"

If I had thought it would have done any good to fall on my knees, I would have done so.

Thor didn't quite look at me. "Don't feel bad, Shanny. I wanted you to tell the truth, and you did."

Oh, but I didn't have to wipe him out there in front of everybody. How could I have been so stupid? Although his words were kind, I felt that he had drawn back from me the same way everybody else had.

"It's a *good* show," Twyla said. "You'll see when we go through it again, Shanny." I wished she would yell at me, be nasty, so I could hate her. How can you fight someone who's *nice*?

She gave another of those piercing whistles for attention, although nobody was making any noise. They were all watching the real-life drama that was going on there in front of them.

"Okay, you guys," Thor said in a fake jovial voice. "As Shanny says, we've got a lot going for us. The singing is good and the dancing is terrific, and Twyla's sets are going to knock your eyes out when they're finished. We're still gonna win!"

Everybody cheered, as if in defiance of me.

"Let's take it from the top," Thor said.

This time I got a little more sense of what the show was about. Actually, it was a show within a show. It was about some kids who were going to do a road show, and it started out with a director—Thor—coaching a chorus line of girls in front of the curtain. He says, "Okay, you've got it. Now bring on the guys, and we'll do their part." Then the girls moan and say, "That's the trouble. There *aren't* any guys." So the director tells them to go to the local Rent-A-Rama and *rent* some guys.

That's when the curtain opens, when everybody's eyes would be knocked out by Twyla's sets, only they weren't done yet. Then there's supposed to be a Rent-A-Rama storekeeper, who wasn't there either, and he was supposed to sing about all the stuff he has there in his store. He says what they need for a show are dancers and singers and costumes, and he shows them all those things. But the girls say no; all they need is guys. He shows them a couple of guys he has, both hunks, but they are both demonstrators and not for rent. The girls ask if he doesn't have some more guys, and he says he has some but they are real rotten eggs, and the girls will have to take them "as is." The girls say that "as is" guys are better than *no* guys, so they take them.

So far, so good. I liked it.

Then the guys come out and do a number about how bad they are, and the girls say they can't do a show with "as is" guys. That's when it all started to break down. There were a lot of long speeches by some mothers, and you not only got your eyes knocked out by Twyla's sets, but you also got clobbered on the head with the moral.

It *was* a bad show, but I wasn't about to tell that to Thor again.

"It's going to be great," I lied when we finished. "All it needs is more rehearsal."

"Next rehearsal is Tuesday night," Thor announced. "DeWitt will be back, and we'll really get down to business."

I was zippering up my drums when he came over to talk to me. "Shanny, I have to stay here and work with Twyla and the sets committee. U Haul is going to drive you home."

I would have been glad to stay and help, too. But I had the feeling I wasn't wanted. Not by the other kids. And not by Thor.

U Haul's car was an old Buick that had fallen on hard times. All of its fenders had rusted through, and its paint job had passed away about ten years back. The trunk was tied shut with a length of rope, and where the back seat should have been there was only a huge bean-bag.

"People are always asking me if anybody was killed

in the wreck," U Haul said as he stowed my drums
inside. "Hope you don't mind risking your life."

"I'll take anything I don't have to push," I said.

U Haul grinned as he opened the front door for me
to get in. "I don't promise anything."

He was making a real effort to be friendly. I liked him
for it, especially since nobody else except Loydene had
said a word to me as I left the hall. I decided I wasn't
going to go to any more rehearsals.

I said as much to U Haul after he settled his enormous
bulk into the driver's seat and we started for Aunt
Adabelle's ranch.

"Wish you'd think it over." U Haul's speech was slow,
and he had what I thought of as a cowboy accent. "Wait'll
you hear ole DeWitt play that music. Give us another
chance, Shanny."

"Give *you* another chance?" I was astounded. "*I'm*
the one who needs another chance, U Haul. I'm the one
who fluffed my lines today."

"Aw, maybe we needed it," U Haul said. "Thor had
us psyched up so we thought we were ready to wipe out
everybody in sight. Maybe we needed a little comedown
so we'll work harder."

"This is really important to Thor, isn't it?" I was
beginning to feel that it was more than just a show to
him.

"Yeah." U Haul rubbed his big hands across the top
of the steering wheel. "See, Shanny, we get made fun
of, here in Wolf Creek. The kids we go to school with
in Pratt are all the time calling us 'hicks from the sticks,'
and they say that to get to Wolf Creek you go as far

back into the hills as you can—then you go a little far-
ther. They say we have one leg shorter than the other
from walking on our steep hillsides. Aw, it's all in fun,
but it gets to us after a while. Thor says we're going to
do a winning show and change our image."

This was familiar territory. I mean, I was as well acquainted with low self-image as I was with the nose jewel
on my face. And I knew all about fighting back, too.
Wasn't that why Flame and I had pulled the Great Dog-
Food Caper?

Was that why? I had never realized it before. I stored
it away to think about later.

"We need you to help us, Shanny," U Haul said. "You're
really great on those drums."

It was nice to be needed.

"Okay, U Haul," I said. "By the way, what's your
real name?"

"Aw, shoot, I was hoping you wouldn't ask." He sort
of ducked his head as he said, "It's Millard, but I'd just
as soon you call me U Haul."

"Right on, U Haul," I said.

He grinned at me as he turned down Aunt Adabelle's long lane, and I gratefully realized that I had a
friend.

After U Haul unloaded my drums and left, I went
looking for Aunt Adabelle. I found her at the kitchen
table, sorting through more old letters. Several of them
were opened and lying scattered around the table.

She looked up as I came in. "How'd it go, Shanny?"
I told her. I didn't leave out anything.

"Pshaw, Shanny," she said, "you probably did them
a favor. It's not easy to make that bunch knuckle down

to real work. Maybe they'll do it now, just to show you up."

"That's about what U Haul said," I mumbled. "But they're sure not going to vote me Miss Congeniality." I didn't mention that Thor wasn't likely to think of me as the love of his life after I hacked him down like that.

"They'll come around if you help them to win."

I sighed. "That's the trouble, Aunt Adabelle. The script falls apart about halfway through, and I'm not sure all the other talent is going to help it that much."

"Then Thor should know," Aunt Adabelle said. "Tell him what's wrong. You're not doing him any favor if you let him go on thinking he's got a big winner."

But people don't like to be told what's wrong. How did I like my folks telling me I was going nowhere and that it was about time I shaped up? I *didn't* like it—that's how much I liked it—and that's how come I ended up here on Aunt Adabelle's ranch.

I didn't want Thor feeling toward me the way I felt toward my folks—any more than he did already.

Sighing again, I said, "Aunt Adabelle, will you explain a couple of things to me? First, just what *is* Pioneer Day?"

"Well, Shanny, it's just a day we've set aside to honor the pioneers who first came to settle in the Great Basin. They entered the Salt Lake Valley on July 24, 1847, so we have some kind of celebration every year on July 24."

That was clear enough. "Okay," I said. "Now would you explain road shows? Ever since I got here people have been talking about winning and all that. I still don't know just exactly what it is we're trying to win."

Aunt Adabelle chuckled, a deep, comfortable sound in her chest. "Isn't that the way it goes? It's all so much a part of us that we expect a newcomer to know all about it." She began to gather up all the opened letters as she spoke. I reached out to help, but she pulled them away from my hands as if she didn't want me to see them. I wondered what could be in a pile of faded old letters that I shouldn't see.

"Road shows," Aunt Adabelle said, "are one of our customs. The church folks sponsor them. You young people might call them mini-musicals. They're fifteen minutes long, and they have to be original, except for the music. But I do believe Thor and DeWitt even wrote the *music* this year."

"That's why I didn't recognize any of it," I said. "But where does the winning part come in?"

Aunt Adabelle folded her letters and stuffed them into an old shoe box that was there on the table, then took the shoe box onto her lap, protecting it with her arms. "Well," she said, "each little town around here prepares its own show, and on the night when they are performed, judges rate them on script and sets and costumes and all that kind of thing. The one that gets the most points is the winner. In these parts, it's something like getting an Academy Award to take first place."

No wonder it was important to Thor. I felt fortified by my new knowledge. Knowing how much was at stake might help me to tell him he needed to work over the last part of the script. And maybe my drums and I *could* help him out.

I let my mind wander to the night of the awards. It was time for the Greatest Contribution of Talent award to be announced. The master of ceremonies would say, "May I have the envelope, please?" He would open it up and say, "The award goes to Shanny Alder for her great work on the drums."

And Thor would rush to my side to gaze into my eyes and say, "Shanny, you're a Genuine Certified Miracle."

On the other hand, couldn't it just as easily go to Twyla for those eye-knocking sets?

With a sigh I went upstairs, where I set up my drums and battered at them for a while in an attempt to get my world back in order. It made me feel a lot better, as always.

From the window I could see Bucky out by the corral, but he didn't come in for dinner. I didn't know whether it was because he was still spooked by what happened at the Bride's House or whether he didn't like Battered Beef, which was what Aunt Adabelle was serving that day.

After Aunt Adabelle and I finished dinner and I washed the dishes, I went upstairs to take a nap. But I was too restless to sleep. The summer, long and Thorless, stretched out ahead of me as dull and dry as the Sahara Desert. Whether I told him his show stank or whether I didn't, I had lost him to Miss Nice Twyla.

Maybe if I proved to my folks that I was shaping up, they might let me go home early, since Aunt Adabelle didn't seem to want me to help her pack. If I wrote them a letter, using one of the stamped, self-addressed envelopes Mom had provided me with so I could write once a week, I could tell them the things I had already learned about myself. Maybe it would convince them that I was trying, and they would say, "Shanny, come home."

I dug out the notebook in which I had written earlier and added a third entry:

3. I usually put my mouth in high gear before my brain even turns over.

Then I read all three entries.

There was nothing there that would bring joy to a parent's heart. I was still a dud. I was strictly "as is."

7

What good would it do to write to my parents and tell them I had "found myself" and that what I'd found just proved I was a dud? That would probably mean permanent assignment to the open-air, blue-skied prison that was Aunt Adabelle's ranch.

What was there to tell about anything? I certainly hadn't made any progress in getting Aunt Adabelle prepared to leave the ranch. I thought about writing about the way she talked with Uncle Vic there at the Bride's House. But that would probably bring Cousin Fayette flying out to investigate, poking her know-it-all nose into everything and bossing me around.

So I didn't write anything. Mom had said, "Mail us one of these each week" when she gave me the stamped, addressed envelopes. I picked up one of them now, licked the flap, sealed it, and took it downstairs and up the long lane to the mailbox. Placing it inside, I raised the little red flag, then ran a finger across the fancy calligraphy that Twyla had done on the mailbox, wishing I could rub it out and her along with it.

Did I really wish that? What had Twyla done to deserve being rubbed out? After all, she had known Thor first. *I* was the troublemaker, the butt-in, the would-be love thief.

Was I that kind of person? What kind of person *was* I? Is it possible to live in the same body for fifteen years and not even know yourself?

Christopher Columbus had nothing on me. I was discovering a new continent, and I didn't know what to call it.

I turned and ran down the lane, as if to escape from myself.

Bucky yelled at me when I arrived back in Aunt Adabelle's yard. "Shanny," he called, "come over here."

He was sitting on the top rail of the corral fence. Blastoff stood a few feet inside the corral, sagging under the weight of his years and the force of gravity.

"I've got a problem," Bucky said.

"Lucky you," I said, "to have just one."

"I've got more than one, but this one's the biggest." He shifted around so he could look at me. "I was just talking to Blastoff. I told him we're going to be in the Pioneer Day rodeo. He's really thrilled about it."

I peered at Blastoff, looking for symptoms of thrill. He returned my peer. Then slowly he turned his back on me, insolently switching his tail as if to get rid of an annoying fly.

I had had better backs than his turned on me that day. "So what's the problem?" I asked.

Bucky sighed. "He won't buck."

"Won't buck?"

Blastoff turned his head so he could watch us with one suspicious eye.

"You can't have a bucking bronco in a rodeo without the bucking," Bucky said. "And Blastoff won't buck. Even when I get on his back and tickle his ribs."

"Couldn't you just ride him around the arena?" I watched Blastoff, who closed his eye as if he were bored with our conversation.

"He'd be embarrassed to have a kid like me ride him when he used to be the meanest horse in the state. So I was just wondering." Bucky stopped and wondered a minute. "I was wondering if you're going to try out for Pioneer Day Queen because if you are, you'll win for sure, and then you could ride Blastoff in the parade." Bucky said the whole sentence fast, as if he were afraid I'd object if he slowed down. "He'd be real excited to carry the *queen*, Shanny. That would be almost as good as showing off how good he can buck. Would you, Shanny? Ride him, I mean?"

"I don't know, Bucky." I wanted to make him happy, but how could I? "I didn't sign up to try out for queen, and besides, I don't know how to ride. I've never been on a real horse in my whole life."

"I can teach you," Bucky said earnestly. "I've been riding horses ever since I was a little kid. And *anybody* can try out for queen, as long as you're a girl."

"Well, okay, Bucky. If I'm picked as the queen, I'll ride Blastoff." I felt safe in promising because I hadn't signed up with the girl, Dot, who had been carrying the clipboard around. Trying out for queen wasn't something I would want to do anyway. It was girls like Cookie

69

Partain back home who entered beauty contests. Cookie tried out for Miss Anything. She had had a nose job and so many other renovations that the guys around school said they were glad they didn't have to pass a true-false test about her.

"If you'll teach me to ride, that is," I added.

Bucky's eyes lit up. "Hey, Blastoff, you hear that?" Pulling a shriveled apple from his pocket, he held it out to the old horse. It looked like the same apple he had offered me a couple of days before.

Blastoff opened a bored eye, then ambled over and took the apple between his thick lips. After tasting it, he dropped it in the dirt. Turning again, he walked over to the watering trough, where he made rude noises as he drank.

"He'll come back and get it later," Bucky said. "He loves apples."

His problem solved, Bucky jumped down from the rail. Taking my hand, he towed me toward the house. "Let's go play Monopoly," he said. "But keep hold of my hand if we see Aunt Adabelle."

So he *was* afraid. "Bucky," I said, "what's the matter? What is it that worries you about Aunt Adabelle?"

He looked sidewise at me, his eyes narrowed. "*You* know."

"Well, I'm not sure I do, Bucky. Aunt Adabelle misses you. She says she wishes you'd come back and watch 'All My Children' with her the way you used to."

Bucky looked at me again, as if he knew something that I didn't. Then he said, "I just love to play Monopoly. I hope I get Park Place and Boardwalk."

Aunt Adabelle wasn't anywhere to be seen when we went into the house to get the Monopoly set. I wondered if she had gone up to the Bride's House again.

We set up our game in the shade of the vines on the wide front porch. I was bringing out some lemonade when I heard a motor coming down the long lane from the highway.

It had to be Thor. He was coming to tell me I was right about the show. He was going to thank me for pointing it out to him, and he was going to say, "I've fixed it." I wouldn't have to worry anymore about it.

But it wasn't Thor. It was Loydene on a dirt bike. She parked it by the lilac bushes on the edge of the lawn and came bouncing up the porch steps.

"Lardy," she puffed, "have *I* got things to tell *you*."

Bucky looked up, clearly annoyed by the interruption. "We was just starting a game. Do you want to play?"

"No. I always go bankrupt." Loydene pulled a porch chair over to the table and sat down. "I'll give you a quarter if you'll get lost for ten minutes, Bucky."

He considered it. "I will for 35 cents."

"Forget it," Loydene said.

Bucky slid off his chair. "Yell when the ten minutes is up." He held out his hand.

Loydene fished a quarter out of a pocket of her jeans and laid it on his palm. Bucky climbed over the railing of the porch and headed for the corral, looking over his shoulder every few feet.

Loydene narrowed her eyes. "What's he feeling so slinky about? Has he done something he shouldn't?"

I didn't know Loydene well enough to tell her how

he was afraid of Aunt Adabelle. "He's probably just playing cops and robbers," I said. "What is it you're going to tell me?"

"Oh, lardy." Loydene turned back to me. "I don't know if we're going to have a road show or not. Thor's come all unglued and says he should have let Sister Davis write the road show in the first place."

"Sister Davis?"

"*Mrs.* Davis. You know how we call each other Sister and Brother in the church. Mrs. Davis is a writer. She sold a story to a magazine in New York in May."

Loydene waited for me to be impressed, and I was. I knew some people at home who sold stories and books, but it wasn't all that easy to do. "That's really good, Loydene."

"She's Dannalee Davis's mother. You know, Dannalee was one of those girls out on the lawn painting scenery."

I couldn't remember which one she was. Loydene went on. She told me that Thor was ready to withdraw the show from the competition altogether rather than go ahead and get another low rating, which I gathered they had always had before.

"Why doesn't he just get Mrs. Davis to help him fix it up?" I asked.

"Well, I guess he would if she was here," Loydene said.

She picked up a handful of little red hotels from the Monopoly box and started setting them up on Marvin Gardens and Ventnor and Atlantic avenues. "But she used some of the money from her story to take Mr. Davis off to Yellowstone Park right after he got his first hay crop in."

"Can't Thor get somebody else to work on the show with him?"

Loydene shook her head. "Nobody else knows beans about writing a road show, which is why we're always on the bottom in the ratings. Besides, Twyla is telling him there's nothing wrong with it. She's got him believing that it's an all-time winner." She built hotels on Pennsylvania Avenue and North Carolina and Pacific as she spoke.

"Well, maybe it *is*. What do *I* know about road shows?"

"Lardy, Shanny, we all know there's something wrong with that show. We want *you* to help him fix it."

"Me!" I stood up so suddenly that I jiggled the table, knocking little red hotels all over the Monopoly board. "I already wiped Thor out once. What's he going to say if I come prancing up telling him I'm going to rewrite his show? Besides, I don't know how to write a show!"

"You've *seen* some, haven't you? I mean, down there in L.A. you must have big-time shows with Broadway stars and all."

"Sure I've seen some. I saw *Cats* just before I came up here. But I don't know how to *write* one." I was feeling kind of sweaty.

"We're not asking you to *write* one, Shanny. Just tell Thor what's wrong and see if you can do something about it. Except for the shows on TV, he's seen only the musicals we do at Pratt High every year. They're real good, but they're not like professional." She leaned across the table. "Your dad's on TV. You must know *something* about what makes a good show."

If I knew something, it was lying limp and unused

among all the other things people had tried to cram into my brain.

I ran a hand across my forehead. "Who would tell Thor that I'm going to do all this advising?"

"*You,*" Loydene said triumphantly as if she had succeeded in talking me into it. "Call him up. Tell him to bring the script over."

I wondered if I could hitchhike back home. I didn't want to get involved in any of this. I was glad when Bucky came back and stood staring at the Monopoly board.

"Hey," he said, "you've been cheating. You didn't have any hotels when I left."

"I don't have any now, either," I said, gathering up the little red game pieces. "Loydene and I were just talking."

"Did you tell her you're going to try out for Pioneer Day Queen?" Bucky asked.

Loydene looked me over. "Well, why not? All of us do. Did you sign up with Dot? Today is the last day. The queen will be picked at the dance next Saturday night."

"I didn't sign up," I said weakly. "I don't even know what you have to do. Is it like a beauty pageant or something? The contest, I mean?"

Loydene laughed. "Lardy no. Every girl who wants to try out makes a pioneer dress, and then we have some judges who decide who looks the most authentic. I'll call Dot when I get back home and tell her you're going to be a candidate."

"I don't have a dress," I protested. "And I don't know

how to sew." I looked over at Bucky. "I guess I won't be able to try out."

Bucky's face fell. "But I *promised* Blastoff."

"Aunt Adabelle can sew," Loydene said.

"But I don't *look* like a pioneer girl."

Loydene waved that aside. "You will when you're all dressed up with a bonnet and all to cover your hair." She got up and walked into the house. "Aunt Adabelle," she called.

"Loydene!" I wanted to tell her I didn't have any intention of trying out for queen. But Loydene wasn't listening. Walking from room to room, then up the stairs, she continued to call. Bucky took off for the corral again, but I followed behind Loydene.

"There's only one place left that she could be," Loydene said, opening the door to the attic. "She doesn't hear so well anymore, so that's probably why she doesn't answer."

Aunt Adabelle was up there in the attic, a big open space among the rafters of the house. It was obviously used for storage, since there were stacks of boxes and pieces of old furniture all around. Aunt Adabelle sat on an old wicker rocker with the contents of one of the boxes in her lap. She was wearing a yellowed lace shawl over her shoulders.

"Mercy," she said as he trooped up the stairs. "Were you looking for me?" She shoved whatever it was she held back into a box and closed the top. Almost guiltily, I thought.

"Shanny's trying out for queen, Aunt Adabelle," Loydene said.

Aunt Adabelle looked pleased. "I was hoping you would, Shanny. Your mother was such a beautiful queen. You could be just as pretty." She stood up. "Well, that means you'll need a dress. I wonder if your mother's old dress isn't still around here somewhere."

"Let's look," Loydene said. She poked at the lock of an old trunk.

"Oh, you don't want to go through all this trash," Aunt Adabelle said. She walked to the stairs and looked back at us. "I'll find it later. Let's go on downstairs now. I've got kind of warm sitting up here."

Loydene didn't seem to notice how odd she was acting. Or maybe that was the way she *always* acted.

We went back to the shady porch, where we drank the lemonade I had made while Aunt Adabelle told us she didn't keep yard goods around anymore. "I only have a passing acquaintance with a sewing machine these days. But if I can't find your mother's dress, we can whip up something. You'll have to get into Pratt and pick out some material, though."

"I'll be going to Pratt on Monday," Loydene said. "I ordered something that will make Thor happy." She grinned. "It's a secret."

I was glad something was going to make him happy because I didn't think he would be too pleased about my messing around with his show the way Loydene wanted me to.

"Mind if I go with you to Pratt on Monday?" I asked. "That is, if we don't find my mom's old dress."

"I was going to ask you to go along with me anyway," Loydene said. "It'll be fun. We'll have a burger at the Polar Freeze and maybe even a chocolate shake."

It sounded like pure bliss.

When Loydene left, I walked up the long lane to the highway with her. I took a pen with me because I wanted to make a change on the letterless letter I was mailing to my folks.

"Don't forget to call Thor," Loydene said as she got on her dirt bike and roared away. "We're counting on you," she called over her shoulder.

I waved to her, then opened the mailbox and took out the empty envelope I had put there earlier. On the back I scribbled, "Dear Mom and Dad, I'm going to try out for Pioneer Day Queen. Love, Shanny."

It would give them hope that I was making progress. I felt the need to be kind to somebody since the next decision I had to make was whether or not to make that phone call to Thor, and I hoped he would be kind to me.

8

For some reason, as I walked back down the lane, I thought of Mark Delaney. He was the student body president of my high school and also a Shakespeare freak. In our assemblies he always used a speech from *Hamlet* when he was trying to prod us on to greater glory on the football field or in speech competitions or on PSAT scores. He would stand up there on the stage in our big auditorium, put a hand on his chest, and say, "This is the question, girls and guys: 'Whether 'tis nobler in the mind to suffer the slings and arrows of outrageous fortune, or to take arms against a sea of troubles and by opposing end them.' " Then he would lean over the lectern and yell, "Don't be floppy discs! Get out there and take arms!"

Our school is loaded with high achievers. You could get trampled to death in the rush of people getting out there to win. But who was going to notice you if you had nothing to win *with*? If you had no talents to speak of and weren't beautiful enough to be Homecoming Queen? If you didn't have the smarts to get out and make a difference in the world? If you never did a single thing that would earn you the right to have Mark Delaney call you by your first name?

Flame said some of us *had* to be floppy discs. Otherwise there would be nobody for the others to achieve *over*. She and I had this idea once that we would organize a club called United Floppy Discs of America. But nobody paid any attention to the signs we put up, and we just sort of sank into obscurity until we decided to go weird. And then of course there was the Great Dog-Food Caper.

Well, maybe now was my chance to "take arms." Maybe I could help the Wolf Creek kids be winners. So what if I was taking a chance of alienating Thor permanently? There are always casualties in every battle.

Before I called Thor, I wrote a long letter to Flame, telling myself Thor probably wasn't home from working on the scenery yet. But I knew I was just stalling, so I took a deep breath and picked up the phone.

Thor's mom answered.

"Thor's not here," she said when I asked to speak to him. "He and Twyla went somewhere. He won't be back until late. Could I have him call you tomorrow?"

"Yes, please," I said. "Have him call Shanny Alder at Aunt Adabelle Spencer's place."

"Oh, Shanny," Mrs. Jorgensen said. "I've been wanting to meet you. Bucky talks about you all the time. He just told me you're going to try out for Pioneer Day Queen and he's sure you're going to win."

I guess there was no way I was going to get out of it

79

if it was already spread all over town. "I hope he's not too disappointed if I *don't* win," I said. "He wants me to ride Blastoff if I'm queen."

Mrs. Jorgensen laughed. "Well, *that* would be real different. We usually make a covered-wagon float like the one your mother rode on the year she was queen."

"Did you know my mom?" For some reason it surprised me. It's hard to realize that there was a world before I was born, one in which my mother was a young girl and walked the same ground I did now and had friends who grew up and had children whom I now knew. I wondered if they ever looked ahead, back then, and thought about their children. I had never given a thought to children I might someday have. Would my children and Thor's children know each other? Would his children and mine be the *same* children? Not likely, the way things were going.

"Of course I knew your mom," Mrs. Jorgensen said. "We went to all the dances together, she and I and all those cousins of hers. And oh, the parties we used to have there at Aunt Adabelle's, with Uncle Vic keeping everybody laughing with his jokes and Aunt Adabelle shoveling out the food."

She gave a little sigh, then said, "You must be a lot like your mother, Shanny. Bucky says you're beautiful."

And Thor? Hadn't *he* said anything about me?

"Bucky's nice," I said. I didn't add that he had odd tastes.

"Yes, he is," Mrs. Jorgensen agreed. "Tell your mother that Ardys Melton says hello. That's the name she would remember me by. And I'll tell Thor to be sure to call you."

After I hung up, I wished I hadn't called. I didn't want to know that Thor was off somewhere with Twyla for the whole evening. If Loydene was right, then Twyla was pumping him full of confidence about the show. He was going to burst like a balloon when I pinpointed his problems.

Aunt Adabelle still wasn't ready to give me anything to do, so I went out and gathered the eggs, then wandered around the big yard and corral and the barn, hearing the echoes of all those parties Mom and The Cousins and Ardys Melton and the others had had. How could Mom have thought my summer would be like hers had been, with all those people around and Aunt Adabelle more than twenty years younger and Uncle Vic alive and being the life of the party? It was like an old abandoned stage set now, with just me and Aunt Adabelle and Blastoff haunting it like leftover ghosts.

When I took the eggs in, Aunt Adabelle asked if I wanted to go with her to the Bride's House to feed Shirley. It wasn't high on my priority list if there had been anything else to choose from, but it was better than watching Saturday afternoon TV. "Sure," I said. "I'll go."

"Bucky usually goes with me," she said. "I just don't know what's the matter with him. He never misses a day of 'All My Children' during the summer, but he hasn't been around now since Thursday. I see him down by the corral now and then, but he doesn't come in."

"Oh, you know how kids are," I said. "He's probably found something else that keeps him busy." I made a mental note to nail Bucky as soon as possible and try to persuade him that Aunt Adabelle was nothing to be afraid of.

Aunt Adabelle took a can from the cupboard and opened it, leaving the lid lying on top as a cover. "I had Thor pick up some cat food the other day," she said. "I figure since Shirley's in the family way, she ought to be getting better nutrition than just scraps."

I had never heard anybody really say "in the family way." I thought people said it only in books. But somehow it seemed right for Aunt Adabelle to use it, since she couldn't even bring herself to write out Sex Appeal in the letters she had sent me. It seemed kind of sweet and caring, and I was touched, too, that she took Shirley's health so seriously.

We started toward the Bride's House, walking around the barn and over the chattery little creek behind it. Blastoff lifted his head when we went by and flapped his big upper lip at us before he settled back into his usual coma. There were long shadows on the rutted dirt road that led up the hill, and somewhere in the trees an owl hoo-hooed.

Aunt Adabelle started to puff before we had gone more than a fourth of the way. "It gets steeper every day," she said. "Seems like just yesterday that I could trot up here without even breathing hard."

"I'll go on up and feed Shirley if you want me to," I offered. "You've already climbed this hill once today."

I hadn't meant to let her know I knew, but Aunt Adabelle didn't seem to mind.

"Yes," she said. "I had to talk something over with Vic. I didn't feel I could wait until Shirley's supper time."

I could feel the little hairs at the back of my neck

quiver, and I wouldn't have been surprised if my hank of purple hair had stood straight in the air like a cat's tail. Aunt Adabelle spoke as if Uncle Vic just sat there at the Bride's House waiting to talk to her whenever she felt the need to visit.

I began to feel a little bit like Bucky and wanted to run back down the hill. But instead I swallowed and said, "Do you really talk to Uncle Vic, Aunt Adabelle?"

"Lands, yes," she puffed. "Vic and I, we lived together for nearly sixty years. He's the only one who understands what it's like for me these days. What it's like to be old and not know quite how you got that way. About how everything is changing so fast you can't keep up with it all. He's all I've got to talk to."

What was I supposed to say? I wished desperately that I had some kind of knowledge about things like this—about old people and how sometimes they get confused and do things that are odd.

"You could talk to *me*, Aunt Adabelle," I said.

Aunt Adabelle panted along in silence for a few steps. Then she said, "Maybe I could, Shanny. Maybe growing old is not so different from growing *up*, with so many things coming at you."

If I could just get her mind away from Uncle Vic, I might be able to get her to start packing to leave the ranch and go where there were people who knew what to do about her problem. "I think the two of us might have a lot in common," I told her.

She nodded. "I'll talk it over with Vic," she said.

When we got to the Bride's House, she invited me inside. But the wind was sort of moaning in the trees and the day had come to that gloomy time when it was neither light nor dark. I didn't feel I was up to a séance, or whatever Aunt Adabelle did to bring Uncle Vic back. I said I would feed Shirley and wait outside.

Shirley wasn't any friendlier this time than she had been before. I scraped the cat food out into a dish Aunt Adabelle kept there and held it toward her. Shirley crouched under the porch, meowing hungrily but making no move to come out. Now that I knew she was pregnant, I could see how her sides pouched out.

"Look," I told her, "you're not doing yourself any good squatting in there while the food and the petting are out here. Come on out and I'll scratch your back while you eat."

My words had a familiar ring to them.

"You're only hurting yourself," I went on. I pushed the food closer. "See what you're missing."

No wonder it sounded familiar. It was the kind of thing my parents said to me. I had squatted there behind my bad grades and goof-off behavior and purple hair while they coaxed me to tune back into the world with verbal tidbits about what I was missing.

But as Aunt Adabelle said about Shirley, I had my reasons, and they had to do with Mark Delaney and all those other movers and shakers. What else is there to do but hide when you're an inadequate in a world of doers?

But sometimes things happen so that you have to do something even if you are still inadequate. Maybe that's how you learn how to deal with the next thing that comes along.

"Okay, babe," I told Shirley. "Stay there if you want

to. But those babies of yours are going to come pretty soon, and then maybe you'll want help." I shoved the food dish under the porch. Remembering a line from an old Humphrey Bogart movie I'd seen on TV, I said, "If you need me, just whistle."

Then I went around to the front of the Bride's House to wait for Aunt Adabelle to finish talking to her dead husband.

I didn't want to go to church with Aunt Adabelle the next day, but she talked me into it.

"You're not going to be any great surprise to anybody," she said when I objected that I had no church-type clothes. "It's all over town that you're a little different, and you might as well go and give them an eyeful. They haven't had so much to talk about since last summer when Fenella Schultz ran off with a linoleum salesman. You're this summer's sensation."

She offered to lend me a dress, but after looking through her closet of flowered polyester dresses, I chose the long-ish khaki skirt I had arrived in, put on my Boy George T-shirt with the front turned to the back, then covered up the back where the picture was with a faded velvet vest.

Aunt Adabelle drove us to church in her trembling old car, which looked to be the same vintage as Blastoff. Its tires were a little squashy, and it jackrabbited going up hills, but it got us there.

Most people were nice to me when Aunt Adabelle introduced me around, although they looked a little startled. Some whispered behind their hands the way the

85

kids had done on Saturday, and I could see Perlie Truesdale's lips forming the word "lardy" every time she looked at me.

All in all, it wasn't too bad until Thor came up to me after the services and said, "My mother said you wanted to talk to me."

"Yes, I do," I said. "Thor, I've had a few ideas about your show and wondered if you'd like to talk them over with me."

"No, it's all right, Shanny." He spoke stiffly as if somebody had starched his lips. "Twyla says it's going to work just fine if we get in a few extra rehearsals. We really don't have time to make any changes. Thanks for being concerned, anyway."

Okay, drop it, I told myself. It was his problem.

But then I thought of U Haul's big face, all bunched up with worry when he wondered what was wrong with the show. And there was Loydene's confidence that I could help them save it.

I propped up my courage to say what I had to say, wishing that instead I could just whip off one of my Esoteric Facts and make him laugh and look at me the way he had on the day I had arrived.

"Thor," I said. "It *isn't* all right. The last part needs a lot of work. Otherwise, those judges will forget how good the first part is. If you're going to leave them with a good impression, you have to have a socko ending."

"The performance is only a week from Saturday," Thor said. He took a step away from me.

"There's time enough," I said desperately. "I've heard my dad say that on TV shows they make changes right up until the taping."

86

"But they can retape if something goes wrong," Thor argued. "We get only one shot at it and that's it."

"Then make it a *good* shot," I said.

"Thanks, Shanny," Thor said, "but I don't want to mess with it." He turned and walked away, over to where Twyla stood with a group of girls, leaving me feeling alone and unwanted.

I told Aunt Adabelle about it as she drove us home. She clucked sympathetically. "Well, I guess it's like they say—win a few, lose a few."

After our Sunday dinner, I went upstairs and wrote a fourth entry in my notebook:

4. You can't win them all.

I looked at it, then added, "But you can't win *any* of them if you don't try."

It was then that I heard a car coming down the lane from the highway. I could tell by the sound that it wasn't Loydene's dirt bike.

It was Thor in his blue pickup with Twyla's thunderbolt on the door. I watched from upstairs as he stopped and got out, holding a sheaf of papers in his hand—his script!

My knees felt weak. "Okay, Shanny," I told myself. "Don't be a floppy disc. Get out there and take arms!"

9

I waited upstairs until Aunt Adabelle called, "Shanny, Thor's here to see you." Even then I took my time going down. After all, there was a chance Thor had come to slam me over the head with that script, and a person doesn't hurry to her own execution.

Aunt Adabelle must have wondered about it, too, because she hovered nearby, questions in her eyes.

But I could tell right away from his sheepish grin that Thor hadn't come to do me in.

He cleared his throat. "Hi, Shanny."

"Hi, Thor." Actually, now that I could see which way it was going to go, I was a little peeved. Not more than an hour earlier he had flicked me off the way Blastoff got rid of an annoying fly and had gone to Twyla. Flame would have told me to make a dramatic scene out of flinging the script in his face and storming back upstairs.

"I've come to apologize," Thor said.

So what did Flame know? She couldn't see him standing there with SUPERHUNK emblazoned on his chest in foot-high letters. Well, not really, but that's the picture that came through my brain waves.

"Apologize for what?" My heart was doing aerobics again.

"For being so far off on an ego trip that I couldn't hear what you were saying."

Aunt Adabelle looked relieved. Putting up a hand to hide a fake yawn, she said, "If you young folks will excuse me, I think I'll go take my Sunday nap." She went upstairs, but then I heard her go on up to the attic.

After she left, Thor said, "I'd really appreciate it if you'd go over this dumb script with me and see what you can suggest."

I could see how hard it must have been for him to cancel that ego trip and come to see me, especially with Twyla whispering in his ear that it was such a good script.

"This is more than just a show to you, isn't it, Thor? I mean, U Haul told me about how you want to create a new image for the Wolf Creek kids."

He seemed grateful that I understood. "I don't know how come I thought I could pull it off. But I took a look at all the talent we've got here and the way DeWitt plays that synthesizer of his, and I thought why not go for it? But I guess my own talent ran dry a little too soon."

Well, now I knew what DeWitt's gadget was. A synthesizer could add a lot to any show.

"Just because you didn't get it right the first time doesn't mean you don't have the talent," I said. "I'll bet DeWitt wasn't any whiz the first time he played the synthesizer."

Thor grinned. "I get the point." He walked over to the kitchen table and spread out the script. "Let's see what we can hack out of this."

I sat down and read the entire script. The whole thing lacked excitement on paper, but I could remember how well the first part of it had translated into action on stage and figured that could stay as it was. It was the second part that bombed out. But how should I know how to fix it?

Thor sat there looking at me so confidently that I ahem-ed a couple of times, then said, "Okay, here's the setup. The girls need guys to do a show and there aren't any, so they go to the Rent-A-Rama to rent some. The high-pressure salesman there tries to get them to cover up the problem with fancy costumes and dancers and loud music because that's what he has in stock. But the girls insist that they only need boys, so he says he has some 'as is' boys. They say they'll take anything and pay for them. The storekeeper yells offstage for someone to bring in the crate of turkeys. So now the audience is all prepared for some kind of surprise when these 'as is' guys come on." I was thinking frantically all during my recap of the show, but I hadn't come up with any ideas.

Thor nodded slowly as he thought over what I had said. "What I've done is just have them come on and do a song and dance about how awful they are and how they like being that way. How can we pep up their entrance?"

Before I could even open my mouth, Thor snapped his fingers. "A crate of turkeys! I've had the storekeeper *say* that. Why don't I use it?" He turned to me, excitement lighting his face. "They'll enter in a crate, with their heads sticking out like a bunch of turkeys. In fact, we can bring them in from the back of the hall, up through the audience to the stage."

He scribbled notes to himself.

"Good," I said. "Now when they get out of that crate, how are they going to act when they see the girls? They've been on the shelf for a long time."

Thor laughed. "They're going to come on to them. They're going to call them 'chicks' and totally gross them out."

Thor was rolling.

"So how will the girls react?" I prodded.

"They turn off," Thor said. "They reject them, and *that's* when the guys go into their 'bad guys' song and dance."

I looked at the script. "Okay, now what you've got is a bunch of mothers coming out and giving them a lecture. I'm not sure I believe that will change them into guys who will cooperate and be in the show. Okay, instead of having them lecture the guys, why don't you have them understand what has *made* them 'as is'?"

I wondered how much of myself I was revealing. Did my mom understand how it was with me?

Thor was scribbling again. "I'll put in a production number for them. They'll love it." He scribbled some more. "I'll work it out. Now we still have one problem. How do we show that the guys change if they don't make these dumb speeches I've got here?"

I closed my eyes, trying to visualize some of the musical revues the super achievers at my high school had put on.

"Costumes," I said. "Have them come in first dressed

in real grungy clothes; then during the mothers' production number they can go out and make a quick change into something spiffy, like white pants and nice T-shirts. You won't have to have anybody say a word. The audience will get the idea."

"I'll have Dannalee color-coordinate them," Thor said. "She's in charge of the costumes." He looked over his scribbled notes and then suddenly threw his script into the air. "Zowee," he said, "I think we can do it!" Leaping to his feet, he danced a little jig, then pulled me up and hugged me. I could have stayed there all day, but he held me out at arms' length. "If you hadn't come along, I would have fallen flat on my face. We *all* would have fallen on our faces."

For a moment I thought he was going to kiss me. He didn't, but it was close enough that I thought it really might happen on some future day.

"That's what would have been the worst," he said, "letting everybody else down. I've been building them up to really believe we can win. This whole 'as is' idea grew out of how we feel about ourselves and how I wanted to change us from 'as is' to real winners."

"You're going to do it, Thor."

Thor had changed during the last hour. No, I don't mean *he* changed. The way I was seeing him had changed. He had become a *person* to me, not just a *superhunk* with Sex Appeal. But now I saw him as one of those people who make a difference in the world—an Achiever—and that was even more intimidating.

Aunt Adabelle found my mom's old pioneer dress while she was up in the attic. She brought it down still wrapped in the tissue paper it had lain in for over twenty years.

"Maybe we can save ourselves a lot of work, Shanny," she said. "Try it on."

Unwrapping it, I found that Dad had described it pretty well. It was made of some kind of soft white material with blue flowers sprinkled all over it. It had lacy sleeves, and there was a bonnet to match, also trimmed with lace.

I felt sort of odd looking at the dress my mom had worn when Dad first saw her. I wondered if she ever thought of that girl and remembered how sometimes she must have felt as if she didn't fit into her world. No, I couldn't imagine my mom ever not fitting in. Even Thor's mother remembered her as the center of all the fun. Maybe that's why she couldn't understand why I *didn't* fit in.

I didn't fit into her dress, either. I was too big for it. I was taller than she had been and bigger around. That surprised me. I mean, you always think of your mom as this authority figure, towering over you, telling you what to do, taking care of you. But then a day comes along when you say, "Don't tell me what to do anymore. I want to do my own thing." But you're still scared, and sometimes all you want to do is crawl onto your mom's lap and suck your thumb. But you don't admit it, even to yourself. And there's this stranger inside your body, which has become strange, too, and you find yourself doing weird things, like the Great Dog-Food Caper, or sometimes really good things, like guiding Thor to do what he didn't think he could do. And you stand away from yourself and ask, "Which is the real Me?"

Well, neither the real Me nor the fake Me was going to wear my mom's dress. That was certain.

"Why, look at that," Aunt Adabelle said, circling around me. "I guess it's true that each generation is getting bigger."

And more confused, I could have added. But all I said was, "I'll get some material when I go to Pratt with Loydene tomorrow, and we'll go ahead and build a new dress. All this lace isn't exactly my type anyway."

Loydene picked me up the next day in a sleek blue Olds Cutlass.

"I thought your mom or somebody would be driving," I said. "Back home I haven't even had Driver's Ed yet."

"My mom's dead," Loydene said, "and Grandma didn't want to go to Pratt today. Besides, I've been driving for over a year. You can get your daylight license at fourteen in Idaho."

I was impressed. "This your car?"

Loydene laughed. "Where would I get a car like this?"

"Some kids have cars like this where I live," I told her.

She revved the engine, and we started up the lane.

"Not here," she said. "This car belongs to my dad. He's into cars. My grandma's always nagging him to spend his money on something worthwhile, like painting our house. She's always saying, 'Lardy, Truman, I might as well go out and live in the chicken coop. It looks better than the house.' And then Dad says, 'Well, now, Mother, maybe that's where you should be, being as you can out-cluck any of those old hens.' "

I remembered that Loydene's grandma was Perlie Truesdale. I kind of cheered for her dad.

"Grandma's a great one for how things look," Loydene said. "She's always picking at me to dress like a lady." She grinned over at me. "You know what, Shanny? I'd like to be just like you."

"Like *me*?"

"You know, dress like you and cut my hair that way and dye part of it purple and have my ears pierced and all."

"Well, why don't you do it?"

Loydene laughed. "Lardy, Grandma would have a *cow*!"

"You think my folks didn't?"

"Did they?"

"Why do you think I got sent here to Aunt Adabelle's ranch?"

"I thought maybe you came because you wanted to."

"No." We were roaring down the highway now, passing patchwork fields and occasionally a house with a big barn nearby. In the background, like the backdrop of a stage set, were wrinkled old mountains covered with sagebrush, like wool on a sheep's back. "No," I repeated. "I was sent here to be reformed, I think." I wondered if Loydene would be shocked.

She was far from shocked. In fact, she looked delighted. "Oh, Shanny, what did you *do*?"

So I told her about the Great Dog-Food Caper. How Flame and I didn't get noticed by the Super Achievers even after we went punk and how we decided one way to attract attention was to do something for the good

95

of the school. There was this PTA meeting that was being held in the cafeteria for the purpose of deciding whether the food was as bad as all of us said it was. Flame and I volunteered to be on the committee to serve the food, and we substituted some dog-food burgers that we had made up beforehand for the real thing. But somebody snitched on us, and we got into all kinds of trouble, with speeches about how we could have poisoned everybody. It was kind of funny, though, because one man said he'd just as soon take a chance on the dog-food burgers as the real ones, so they made some changes and the food did improve a little.

"Didn't you even get credit for that?" Loydene said indignantly.

"Well, yes, I guess so. But mainly it just started a new thing of everybody barking when they saw us. Then I got sent here."

"I'm real glad you came, Shanny."

"So am I, Loydene."

It was true. For the first time since I had come, I was glad I was there rather than back in California on the beach with Flame.

Pratt wasn't any bigger than I remembered it, but at least it had stores. There were people, too, and I got some strange looks. One man about broke his neck craning around to stare at me and then ran into a lamppost.

It didn't bother Loydene to be seen with me. She seemed to like it.

I had been thinking for days about having a big Slurpee when I got into town, but Pratt didn't have any

7-Eleven stores. I settled for a cheeseburger, fries, and a chocolate milk at the Polar Freeze.

"Lardy, I love junk food." Loydene sighed as we ate. "I hardly ever get to have any."

"Flame and I eat it almost every day at the beach," I said, thinking maybe that was why I was a lot heavier than my mom had been at my age. I was surprised to learn that I didn't enjoy the burger as much as I had planned to. Maybe it was the memory of the dog-food burgers that was sticking in my mind. Or maybe it was because I had come to like Aunt Adabelle's cooking a lot. Even though she called it funny names, it was good.

"Is your girl friend's name really Flame?" Loydene asked, swallowing the last of her onion rings.

I shook my head. "It's Virginia, but she says if you want to be an exciting person, you should call yourself by an exciting name."

"I should call myself Storm," Loydene said. "Maybe I'd dare stand up to Grandma." Wiping her hands on her napkin, she stood up, looking at her watch. "We have just enough time to do our errands before the bus comes in."

"Bus?"

"Oh, I guess I forgot to tell you. DeWitt's coming back on the bus today, and I told his mom I'd fetch him home."

So I was about to get better acquainted with the famous DeWitt, who possessed the wonderous talent on the synthesizer.

Loydene took me to a yard-goods store, where we picked out some golden brown gingham for my pioneer dress. She said I would be a knockout in that color and would have a good chance at being named Pioneer Day Queen.

"Are you trying out?" I asked, not wanting to overstep my territory now that I had come to like Loydene so much.

"Oh, sure," she said. "But I'll never win."

I could tell that she would like to, though.

"I won't win either," I said.

Loydene gave me a pixie grin. "It's not over yet, Shanny," she said.

Our next stop was a store where Loydene's brother-in-law was the manager. He brought out a big box and a little bill.

"I'm losing money on this deal, even if these *are* seconds," he told Loydene. "If I weren't an old Wolf Creeker, I wouldn't do it."

"Just consider it your contribution to our new image, Herb," she said as she paid him. "And to the person responsible for it."

"How *is* Thor?" Herb asked, ringing up the sale.

"Well, he's going to be a lot better when he sees what I've got here." Loydene tapped the top of the box with a finger.

So this was the surprise she had been talking about the last time I had seen her.

"What's *in* the box?" I asked as we went back out on the street and headed for the car. "It must be Thor's surprise."

"Well, it's not going to be a surprise if I show you," Loydene said. "I want to surprise *everybody*." But then she giggled. "Lardy, I never could keep a secret. I can't wait to show you."

When we got to the car, she opened the box and held up a white T-shirt. On the front of it was a big "I" and a heart and a thunderbolt, like this: I ♥ ➤➤

"I love . . ." I read. Then I realized what it said. "I love Thor."

"I've got enough for each girl to wear one," Loydene said. "It'll blow Thor's mind. And this way nobody will need to feel like it's True Confession time."

"True Confession time?"

"Lardy, Shanny, every girl in Wolf Creek is in love with Thor. This way we can all say it and not be embarrassed."

A slow flush crept up over my face. How stupid I had been to think that Twyla and I were the only ones in competition for Thor! How naive I was to think he might ever take me out! I might as well wish for Bruce Springsteen to come knocking at my door.

"It's a neat idea, Loydene," I managed to say. "Thor will be pleased."

By the time DeWitt's bus came—and he almost got back on it when he saw me waiting there—I was Shanny the Shameless again. Shanny the Strange. Shanny the Summer Sensation.

10

I had Loydene drop me off on the highway by Aunt
Adabelle's lane. I wanted to check the mailbox in case
Bucky hadn't come for the mail, and besides, I didn't
think DeWitt could survive many more minutes of my
company. He had sat ramrod straight in the corner of
the back seat behind Loydene all the way to Wolf Creek.
I got the impression that he expected me to vault over
the seat any minute and attack him. He hadn't said
anything all the way except that, yes, it was a nice day
and that his grandmother in Pocatello was fine except
for her gall bladder. Now and then I looked back at
him, trying to include him in the conversation, and each
time I caught him staring owlishly at me through the
thick lenses of his glasses.

I didn't tell him that he and I were supposed to be a
team, the musical accompaniment for Thor's road show.
I figured I'd let Thor break the news to him.

"Remember," Loydene said just before she drove off,

"you're going to help me hand out the T-shirts tomorrow night at the rehearsal. Come backstage right after the first run-through."

"Okay," I agreed, noticing that DeWitt looked alarmed. He probably hadn't even realized that I was going to be in the show.

Loydene stepped on the gas, then stopped again. "And listen, if you need help with your queen costume, give me a buzz."

DeWitt's eyes widened so far that I thought he might collapse in on himself, like a black hole. I wondered if he was going to go home and hide until I left town.

"Thanks," I told Loydene. "I'll probably need a lot of help."

Sewing was the first class I ever flunked. My mom made me take it in junior high. I think she had visions of me whipping up little frocks for myself and maybe even a robe or a pair of jeans for her now and then, the way Patti Perfect who lives next door did. Her name isn't really Patti Perfect, but that's what Flame and I call her because she could qualify for the title of Miss God.

There were two letters for me in the mailbox, along with a magazine and a bill for Aunt Adabelle. One letter was from my parents and the other was from Flame.

I could hardly wait to open the one from Flame, but I decided to save it for last. That way if Mom and Dad sent ten pages of advice and reminders to make something of myself, I could wipe it all out with Flame's letter.

I opened the letter from my parents and read it as I walked down the long lane. It wasn't quite what I expected. It was cheerful and full of newsy little items. My mom told about backing her car into our trash cans on her way to work, spilling empty TV dinner boxes out right in front of Patti Perfect's mother, who's into health food and jogging. "She stared at those dead cartons as if they were going to reach out and whammy her cholesterol," Mom wrote. Dad told about how he had just signed to do another pickle commercial and said he'd rather stick with the pickle company than become known as the sinus drainage man like his best friend, Bud.

Mom ended the letter telling about a scrapbook she had kept while she was at the ranch. "It's probably up in the attic in a box with my name on it," she said. "It's not important, but if you can find it, I'd like to remember what those years were like."

They didn't say anything about the empty envelope I had sent to them, so I assumed they hadn't received it yet. I was kind of ashamed about it now that they had written such a nice letter. I wondered if I should call them and say there just hadn't been anything to tell except the bit about trying out for Pioneer Day Queen that I had written on the back.

But I decided not to call. When they got the envelope, they would sigh and say it was just like me to do something like that. So the best thing to do was probably to write them a decent letter and let them think I had made terrific progress in the week between the two.

I saved Flame's letter until I was up in my room, with my shoes off, lying on my bed. I hadn't seen Aunt Adabelle anywhere and wondered if she had gone up to the Bride's House again.

"Dear Shanny," Flame wrote. "Biggie WOW! Three,

count 'em, *three* guys already! What are their names? Which one is it who's in love with you? *Tell* me about him. Does he ride big prancing horses? Is he the one your aunt said has S.A.? Do you think one of the others would like little ol' ME?????"

I had to think a minute to remember what I had written to her the first night I was at the ranch. The three guys had to be DeWitt, Thor, and Bucky—the one who was in love with me. What could I tell her about him or the horse he rode? Would she believe an eight-year-old on a cartoon horse?

She told me about her latest efforts to attract the attention of the lifeguard with the dragon on his chest. "I sat right in front of his station and rubbed oil all over myself," she wrote. "I thought of staging a drowning, too, but figured with all that oil I'd squirt right out of his arms. Besides, he was drooling over a blond whose sunglasses were bigger than her swimsuit."

At the end of her letter she had written F-A-C-T with an arrow pointing to where she had written, "*Did you know* that in 1977 a woman in Texas was buried seated at the wheel of her baby-blue Ferrari?"

Putting down the letter, I lay there in the dim coolness of my room and thought that Flame had about as much chance of catching that lifeguard's eye as I did of getting a date with Thor. What was it, I wondered, that some girls had that made the guys go after them? Why didn't Flame and I have it? How could we *get* it? What *was* it?

Outside I heard Bucky calling me. "Shanny," he yelled. "Are you back?"

Sighing, I put my shoes back on and went downstairs to the only male who wanted me.

"Shanny," Bucky said when I joined him on the top rail of the corral fence, "when do you want me and Blastoff to give you your first riding lesson? You're going to need a few days to practice before you're the queen and ride him in the parade."

I hooked my heels over one of the lower rails the way Bucky did and looked at Blastoff. It didn't seem as if he was any more thrilled about a riding lesson than I was. His ears flopped back on his head, and he watched me with unblinking eyes, like a snake.

"Bucky," I said, "maybe I won't get to be the queen. There are a lot of girls trying out."

Bucky looked at me. "Not any of them are as pretty as you."

I needed that right then. "Thanks, Buck. But I don't have my dress yet. That's the main thing they judge on. And I can't even sew. Maybe I can't make a nice dress."

"Aunt Adabelle will help." His eyes slid toward the Bride's House. "She can probably make a real pioneery dress."

"Is she up there, Bucky? At the Bride's House, I mean? I couldn't find her when I got home from Pratt."

This time he didn't look at me. "Yeah, she's up there. She came while I was there talking to Shirley." Suddenly he turned to face me. "Hey, you know what? Shirley lets me pet her now. I've been up there a lot lately, and her and I have got to be good friends."

"Is that where you've been spending your time, Bucky? Aunt Adabelle keeps asking me if I've seen you. She says you're missing some really good episodes of 'All My Children.' Did you talk to her when she came up to the Bride's House?"

He turned away, but I reached out and put my hand under his chin, making him look at me.

"No," he said. "I ran."

It was time to get to the bottom of this. I had to find out what was bothering Bucky.

"Why did you run, Bucky? Are you afraid of Aunt Adabelle?"

His eyes slid away from mine, and he shook his head.

"Bucky?"

"I'm afraid of *him.*"

"Him?"

"The dead guy she talks to."

"You mean Uncle Vic?"

Bucky nodded.

"But you weren't afraid of him until that day you and I both went up there with Aunt Adabelle. Why are you afraid of him now?"

Bucky shook his chin loose from my hand. "Well, *before* I didn't really think about how he's *dead.*"

So it had been my words that had scared him. But why?

"Bucky," I said, "you were up there at the Bride's House alone today. Weren't you scared then?"

Bucky gazed out at Blastoff, who seemed to have dozed off, his eyes still open.

"*He's* not there when *she* isn't," Bucky said. "See, I had to go up there last week to see how Shirley was, and I *was* afraid, so I called to Uncle Vic to see if he was there. I even looked in through the window. But he wasn't there. I think maybe he stays with *her* because sometimes I've heard her talking to somebody in the attic." He said the last sentence in a low whisper that made little creepy things scamper up my backbone.

"Bucky, *why* are you afraid of Uncle Vic?"

But he didn't answer. He straightened up, pointing toward the road that led from the Bride's House. "There *she* comes," he said. Without another word, he slid from the rail and ran off toward home.

I looked up to see Aunt Adabelle coming slowly down the road, picking her way carefully around the ruts and rocks, moving as if it was painful to walk.

I knew she had been up there at the Bride's House talking with Uncle Vic again and that she would freely admit it if I asked her. She was beginning to spend more time there. Should I tell Mom about it now so that she could consult with The Cousins and they could have her taken away?

No, first I wanted to get Thor to keep his promise about going up there with me when she was there to see if we could figure out what was going on. But wouldn't that be spying?

As for right now, I could go walk with her, to make sure she didn't trip and fall or anything.

I jumped down from the rail and hurried along the narrow little road.

When we got back to the house, I showed Aunt Adabelle the golden brown gingham Loydene and I had bought in Pratt that morning.

Aunt Adabelle held it up against me. "Why, you'll be the prettiest girl at the dance, Shanny. This goods makes your skin look warm and golden, and it brightens up your hair."

I laughed. "Bucky is sure I'll be picked as the queen, and if I am, he wants me to ride Blastoff in the parade. Do you think I could ride him?"

"Why sure, if you want to. It would make Bucky right happy, and it would give the old horse something to think about besides his aches and pains. I think it would be real nice, Shanny."

For the first time I actually *wanted* to be chosen as the queen. And maybe if I could get Aunt Adabelle involved in making my dress, she would forget about trudging all the way up to the Bride's House every day to talk with Uncle Vic.

But then maybe she would go talk with him in the attic, right there in the house.

I didn't sleep well that night. I lay in the darkness listening to Blastoff thud around his corral, performing for his phantom audience. I thought of the dusty, gloomy attic above me with its bare rafters and the old trunks filled with Aunt Adabelle's past and things my mother had owned as a young girl and maybe the ghost of Uncle Vic.

I couldn't blame Bucky for being spooked.

Aunt Adabelle's sewing machine wasn't even electric. She made it go by rocking a little iron platform underneath it with her feet. A treadle, she called it.

"My lands, the miles this thing has sewed," she said, trying it out to make sure it would still work. "We used to keep it going night and day when your mother and The Cousins lived here."

I liked the machine. It seemed friendlier than those whirring terrors we used in junior high that tore the cloth out of your hands and chewed it up faster than you could feed it to them. This one munched along slowly, as if it had all the time in the world. You couldn't be afraid of losing a hand to a polite machine like that.

"Never did take to those electric ones," Aunt Adabelle said comfortably.

"Me either," I said, and knew I wouldn't be writing to Mom yet about Aunt Adabelle's freak-outs. I didn't want her to leave the ranch—not right yet.

The next day Aunt Adabelle and I wrestled with the flimsy pattern for my dress and got all the pieces cut out. By the time I had to get ready for the road-show rehearsal, we even had the bodice sewed together except for the trimmings and the buttons. Aunt Adabelle hadn't had a chance to go up to the Bride's House all day. I called Bucky to tell him to go feed Shirley until further notice. I felt we had made progress in several directions.

Thor called to say that there was some kind of problem with the scenery and that he was going early to help Twyla solve it. I wondered if Twyla had arranged the problem, just to keep him from coming to get me. It didn't matter a whole lot since I didn't have any hopes of being singled out by him since Loydene told me about the T-shirts and how all the girls loved him.

I called Loydene, and she came to pick up me and my drums in her dad's Olds.

"Remember to come backstage after the first run-through," she reminded me. "Lardy, is Thor going to be surprised."

I thought of that big box of I ♥ ⚡ T-shirts, and

108

for some reason felt a little uneasy. I hoped Loydene's surprise wouldn't backfire in some way.

But how could it?

I knew things weren't going to be all good that day when the first thing I did when I was setting up my drums was trip over the electric cord that supplied juice to DeWitt's synthesizer. It died right in the middle of a song he was playing through for Thor, and the noisy hall was suddenly silent.

I heard somebody groan, "Oh, no, not *her* again."

DeWitt climbed up on his bench and stared at me as if I were a snake coiled to strike. I suspected he was on the verge of snatching up his synthesizer and going home.

Then suddenly Twyla was there, spreading Nice all over everybody.

"Shanny didn't mean it," she said, plugging the cord back into the socket. "There's no harm done." Picking up one of my drums, she began to attach it to its stand. "Now take your places everybody. Wait'll you see the incredible changes Thor and I have made."

Like a klutzy kindergartner whose understanding teacher has saved her skin, I scurried to set up my drums, hardly noticing that Twyla was sharing credit for the revised road show.

11

Twyla gave a couple of her sharp whistles to get everyone's attention, and Thor announced that the last half of the show would have to be read since he had just handed out the revised scripts and there hadn't been time to memorize them.

"I'm not sure the changes are as incredible as Twyla says, but I hope you're all happy with them." He grinned at us. "Now, let's go."

He didn't mention my part in the revisions. Well, why should he? All I had done was urge him on while *he* made the changes. For all I knew, he might have gone to Twyla later, and they may have changed the whole thing again.

I didn't have time to think about it anyway because DeWitt climbed down off his bench and, after a suspicious glance at me, went into the introductory music. I struggled to keep up.

There was all the difference in the world in that day's rehearsal and Saturday's. Some of Twyla's scenery was on stage, and I could see how it was going to look like a store with people standing in the compartments and things on the shelves. DeWitt's synthesizer made a strong, full sound that made it seem like show biz. People acted with enthusiasm. Cues were picked up. Bill Jacobson was a funny, funny storekeeper with his booming voice and high-pressure sales tactics. The tap dancers were bright and crisp. And everybody really laughed when the "as is" guys were brought in covered over by an enormous, hastily built crate.

Even DeWitt got carried away, and during a brief break he turned to me and said, "Hey, this is *good*."

Then I guess he realized to whom he was speaking because his eyes got owly again, and he shifted a little on his bench as if to get as far from me as possible.

Even the last half of the show, where people had to read their new parts, was fast and funny. The mothers loved what Thor had put in for them. When the storekeeper started telling the girls what a bunch of turkeys they had bought, how they had no ambition and no talent and no *anything*, Thor had one of the mothers in the audience stand up and yell, "Sir! Sir! I'm sorry to interrupt, but you're going about this all wrong."

Then another mother jumped up and said, "Yes. If you tell them that's what they *are*, that's what they'll be."

A third mother, a tall, chesty lady, leaped up and yelled, *"Have you hugged your kid today?"*

They all pushed their way up on stage and said the

111

words to their new song about "Different strokes for different folks," and that was when the "as is" guys were to go offstage and change their costumes.

There was another short break after the mothers went through their part so that Thor could give some stage directions. While he waited, DeWitt looked over at me again. He didn't say anything this time, but I decided I might as well be friendly. Leaning toward him, I said, "Did you know that in 1977 a woman in Texas was buried seated at the wheel of her baby-blue Ferrari?"

DeWitt stared at me in horror. "Was she dead?" he whispered.

"All *right*," Thor yelled. "Let's move into the *finale!*"

DeWitt was still staring at me. I wished I hadn't said anything. He might yet grab his synthesizer and bolt, leaving us with nothing but drums. When would I learn to keep my mouth shut?

"DeWitt," Thor said. "How about the finale music?"

DeWitt swung around and hit the keys, and we were off into a peppy finale. Somebody had been working on the choreography, and everyone was moving with purpose now.

There were cheers when we finished, and people surrounded Thor, congratulating him on the rewrite. He moved to the edge of the stage, holding up his hands for silence. Twyla followed as if she were attached to him by a string.

"Listen, everybody," Thor said. "Now that you've seen how much better the show is with the changes, I want to tell you that we have Shanny to thank for it. She's the one who saw what was needed and told me what to do."

There was a little silence as if people couldn't believe what he was saying. Then U Haul shot a fist into the air and yelled, "Yay, Shanny!" Other people took it up, and pretty soon I was pushed onstage along with Thor and Twyla. Twyla's nice smile didn't waver as she reached over and squeezed my hand.

Thor wasn't through. "And did you notice what Twyla has added?" He walked over to the half-finished scenery and pushed open a door in back of one of the compartments. "The display dancer will be standing here on the shelf," Thor said. "Then when the storekeeper tries to sell the dancers, the others will come onstage through this door."

It was a neat touch. So Twyla had made some good changes, too. Matching my smile with hers, I reached over and squeezed *her* hand.

We had a longer break then, between run-throughs. I hurried backstage to help Loydene hand out the I ♥ ⚡ T-shirts. Several kids reached out to touch my arm or pat my back and tell me how glad they were about the changes. "Way to go, Shanny," one girl said.

Loydene was busily distributing the T-shirts from a small table back in a corner. Girls were giggling as they read them and stripped off their own shirts to put on the new ones.

"Now don't go out where he can see you," Loydene whispered. "We don't want him to get a preview before the main event."

Twyla walked around her scenery and looked at us. "What's going on here?"

"Have a T-shirt," I said, shoving one at her. "It's a little surprise for Thor."

113

Twyla took the T-shirt and held it up, examining it. "Oh, Shanny," she said, "I don't think Thor is going to like this."

The uneasy feeling I had had earlier took root and burst into full bloom. I knew some guys would be mortified by having twenty girls walking around advertising their love for them across their chests. I didn't know Thor well enough to guess if he was one of them.

"I'm not going to wear this," Twyla said.

"Oh, come on," Loydene urged. "Thor will love it."

Twyla handed the shirt back to me. "I'm sorry, Shanny. I don't want to take part in this."

"What's wrong with it?" Loydene demanded. "It's all in fun."

Twyla ducked her head a little as if she didn't want to say what was wrong with it. Then with a glance at me she turned toward Loydene and whispered, "It's so *tacky.*"

Loydene snorted. "Lardy, Twyla, don't be such a wet rag." She beckoned to four girls who had been listening to the conversation. "Come on and get your shirts. They're free."

One girl drifted toward Twyla, but the others went over and got their shirts.

"Okay, you guys," Thor bellowed from the front of the stage. "Let's get moving. I want to get through the whole thing at least twice more."

"Now, we're all going out at once," Loydene told us. She looked at me. "Lardy, Shanny, aren't you going to change to a Thor shirt?"

It was too late to back out, even if I was worried

about what Twyla had said. I yanked off my Boy George shirt and replaced it with the Thor one.

Several girls giggled nervously as we filed out onto the stage. Loydene herded us into a long, straight line.

"Let's have the chorus line first," Thor said, jumping offstage and turning to face us. "What's this? Is everybody going to be in the chorus line now?" He was going to say more, but looked puzzled as his eyes moved down the long line of identical T-shirts. He turned around to look at the guys who had stopped throwing the basketball and horsing around in back of him. They were staring at us, too. Slowly Thor turned back, his face serious.

"Whose idea was this?" he asked.

Nobody said anything.

Twyla had been standing at the side of the stage. Now she moved forward. "Shanny's modest, so I'll tell you that we have her to thank for *this*, too."

Thor nodded and slowly climbed the steps onto the stage. With his eyes fastened onto mine, he walked over to me.

What was he going to do to me? Would anybody stop him if he began strangling me right there on the stage?

Stopping in front of me, he said, "Shanny Alder," in a deep voice. "Shanny Alder, I am going to hit you with the title of President of the Thor Jorgensen Fan Club." An enormous grin split his face. "I love it, you crazy nut!" Grabbing my hand, he pulled me forward. "Hey, you turkeys," he yelled to the guys out in front, "don't you wish *you* had a fan club?"

"Thor," I said, yanking at his arm. "Thor, it wasn't

my idea. It was Loydene's. *She's* the president of your fan club."

He grabbed Loydene, too, and hugged us both, dancing us around the stage as the other kids cheered. Over his shoulder I could see Twyla, and for the first time since I had known her, I saw she was skating on very thin Nice.

The rest of the rehearsal was fun. During a rest break somebody yelled out, "Hey, Shanny, how about more fascinating facts like you told us on Saturday?"

I didn't repeat the Ferrari one because I didn't want to alarm DeWitt again.

"Okay," I said. "Did you know that the *Encyclopaedia Britannica* has over 43 million words?"

"So does Loydene," a guy yelled.

"Lardy," another guy said, "is that *all?*"

"Okay, you nerds," Loydene said. "You're just jealous because I didn't get T-shirts with *your* names on them."

Everybody was in a good mood, except for Twyla. She moped around the back of the stage, smiling her Nice smile, which now kind of sagged around the edges. I noticed that she had put on one of the T-shirts.

Thor's mother came up and introduced herself to me. She was one of the women who were doing the mothers' number. "That was a nice thing you did for Thor," she said. "He's been so up and down about this show that I know he appreciates the vote of confidence."

I could feel myself blushing a little. I mean, it's sort of embarrassing to have a guy's *mother* around when you're trying to make it with him. "He has a lot of talent," I mumbled. I cleared my throat. "By the way, my mom says to tell you hello."

Mrs. Jorgensen smiled. "She was such a good friend when we were girls. I'd like to see her again. Did you know that you're so much like her I can hardly believe it?"

Like my mother? I couldn't believe it, either, not then and not the next day when I told Aunt Adabelle about it.

"Well, you *are*," she said, treadling her old sewing machine and stitching together more of my dress. "You're creative and adventurous and pretty and fun just the way she was."

"Me?" I said. "Are you talking about *me*?" I stood by her side, thumping myself on the chest every time I said *me*.

"Don't you even know yourself?" Aunt Adabelle said.

"Not if that's what I'm like," I admitted.

Aunt Adabelle chuckled as her needle strolled down the seam of my long pioneer skirt. "Well, I can understand that, too. It takes a while to get to know yourself when you're growing up. But someday you'll see yourself the way I do, and you'll love that Shanny as much as I do."

I felt a hotness behind my eyelids as if I might cry. "Thanks, Aunt Adabelle." For the first time I put my arms around her shoulders and hugged her to me. She felt soft and kind of fragile. "And thanks for making my dress. I've never had a pioneer dress before."

Aunt Adabelle turned a little on her chair so that she could hug me back. "I'm glad to do it, honey. It's been a long time since anybody needed the kind of things I

117

can do. I just hope my hands aren't so shaky that I'll mess it up."

"You're doing a terrific job," I reassured her.

I was still marveling at the things she saw in me. I wished my parents could see the same things.

Thinking of my parents made me remember their letter.

"Aunt Adabelle," I said, "my mom wants me to look for that old scrapbook she kept when she lived here. She said it's probably in the attic. Do you mind if I go up and look?"

I wasn't anxious to go to the attic after what Bucky had told me, but I figured it wouldn't be too spooky in the morning.

"Oh, mercy." Aunt Adabelle half stood. "It's such a mess, Shanny. Dust all over everything. Why don't you let me look for it when I go up there?"

"I don't mind the dust." I decided I really wanted to go up there. Maybe I could find some clue to Aunt Adabelle's behavior. "Why don't I go up there right now and look for the scrapbook? That'll get me out of your hair while you sew."

For a moment I thought she was going to say I couldn't go. But then she sighed and said, "Well, I guess you'd better go now before it heats up from the sun. Your mother's box is probably in the east gable. That's where the girls used to keep their things."

I could hear the soft chatter of her sewing machine as I climbed the stairs, but it stopped when I opened the attic door—almost as if she were listening. For what?

I almost chickened out. Now that I could see the shadows up there, I was scared. I crept up the stairs one at a time, expecting any minute to have a musty ghost sweep down from the rafters and grab me.

Sunlight poured through the small windows of the two gables, and when I turned on the bare light bulb that hung in the center of the attic, the shadows disappeared.

Taking a trembly deep breath, I moved around the stacked boxes. I came to the wicker rocker where Aunt Adabelle had sat the day I had come up there and she had hurried me back down before I could see what she was doing.

Spread on a small table in front of the chair were dozens of photographs. They seemed to be sorted into categories. There were old-fashioned baby pictures and pictures of a young girl. There were wedding pictures and pictures of a man and woman and of the house in which I was standing. There were pictures of an old couple, then pictures of an older woman alone.

On the floor at the end of the table were some scattered brochures that I remembered as the ones about the retirement home that Mom had sent before I came. There was also a stack of yellowing dresses, some of which I recognized from the photographs.

The pictures were all of Aunt Adabelle and Uncle Vic. As I stood there looking at them, I realized that she must have been reviewing the script of her life. And from the way the brochures about the retirement home were dumped on the floor, I got the idea she might have been trying to revise the last part, the way Thor and I had revised his road show.

119

12

I found the box with my mother's name on it pushed far back in the angle where the slanting roof met the floor. There were four pasteboard boxes there, each marked with a name: Jean, Fayette, Rosemary, and Lila. The Cousins—the girls who had filled the old ranch house with fun and parties and guys during the summers they had spent with Aunt Adabelle and Uncle Vic.

Now there were just the boxes and a silent, empty, lonely old house and Aunt Adabelle who didn't want to leave it.

I separated the box marked "Lila" from the others and started to open it. Then I stopped. I didn't want to stir up Mom's girlish memories there in the attic. It was full of Aunt Adabelle—the past, which she had been trying to sort through with all those pictures, and the future, with those brochures from the retirement home.

Turning out the attic light, I carried the box downstairs to my bedroom, where I put it on the little claw-foot table by the windows.

The flaps of the box were brittle, and little pieces broke off as I folded them back and looked inside. The first things I lifted out were a fringed leather vest and a pair of cowboy boots. I guess Mom didn't think she would be using them away from the ranch. Next there was a deep red dish, the kind you get from knocking over a stack of bottles at a midway. There was a tri-angular green felt banner that said YELLOWSTONE PARK, and underneath that was the scrapbook Mom had men-tioned.

Carefully I lifted it out and opened it. The first several pages were filled with pictures of Mom and The Cousins. Some had a shiny Chevy in the background, which I realized with surprise was the same jackrabbitting old wreck that Aunt Adabelle had driven to church. I even found a picture of Blastoff as a proud young horse—the pride of Wolf Creek and the meanest bucking horse in the state of Idaho.

After the pictures were postcards and pressed flowers and snips of hair neatly identified as to the owner. There was a program from the famous Pratt Night Rodeo, which listed the names not only of the cowboys but also the horses. There were notes after the names in Mom's handwriting. Skip DeMars had ridden Arsenic for the required eight seconds. Red Fulton had let go of Slippery Sam after six seconds. And Blastoff had bucked Bill Nordstrom off in three seconds flat.

"Way to go, Blastoff," I whispered, feeling pleased that he had performed so well on that long-ago night.

121

The last page in the scrapbook contained only one thing. It was a lump of something grayish, captured inside a piece of plastic wrap and taped to the page. Underneath was written, "Gum I was chewing the first time Ray kissed me."

Ray—my dad.

I closed the scrapbook, feeling as if I had been walking through somebody else's life—somebody I hardly recognized. My mom hadn't been Lila Alder, Investment Counselor then. She had been just Lila Jennings, Girl Teen-ager, like me. Did she have somebody back then to bug her to Make Something of Herself? How *had* she made that gigantic leap from a silly young girl who saved a wad of gum to the successful businesswoman whose advice people asked for? It wasn't just that time had passed. Time had passed for Old Blastoff, too, but he was still the same, except older.

So even if you did *nothing*, you were going to change, if only to get older. But how did you get to be a Worth-while Person if you didn't have any natural talents that way? And what was the use if you were just going to end up in a retirement home anyway?

"Shanny."

Aunt Adabelle was calling me from downstairs.

"Shanny, come on down and try your dress on before I do the finishing."

I tucked Mom's things back inside the box. If only building a life were as simple as making a dress! You picked out the pattern you wanted, cut out the material, and when you sewed up the seams the way they were supposed to be, *voilà*! There was a dress.

Aunt Adabelle had everything done except for the buttons and hem and some of the lace. She had made some adjustments that she had learned to do from experience, like gathering more of the material in the back of the skirt than in the front so it sort of swept out behind me as I moved. She had added more lace to the neckline and belled out the ends of the sleeves, making lace inserts that gathered at my wrists. And the bonnet was really cute, especially when I tucked my hair up under it so you couldn't see the purple.

"Why, I guess I still have the knack," Aunt Adabelle said, standing back and surveying me when I put the dress on. "You're as pretty as a picture."

The nice thing was, I *felt* pretty as a picture. I had never worn a dress like that before, and in it now I felt pretty and graceful and *womanly*. I wished Thor could see me.

Thor *would* see me. The square dance was on Saturday night, and he was sure to be there. Why couldn't history repeat itself? Why couldn't I become Pioneer Day Queen like my mom, and why couldn't Thor fall in love with me?

"I love it," I told Aunt Adabelle, and kissed her soft, wrinkled cheek, remembering as I did so the pictures of her as a young girl that were spread across the table in the attic.

I wrote a long letter to my folks that night, telling them about Bucky and Blastoff and Shirley and Loydene. I told them about the road show and how the kids expected me to know something about show biz since Dad was on TV.

There were some things I didn't tell, such as how I felt about Thor and about Aunt Adabelle and how she talked with Uncle Vic at the Bride's House.

She was up at the Bride's House when I got up the next morning. She came back while I was making pancakes for the two of us.

"I'm sorry I took so long," she apologized. "I just had so many things to talk with Vic about. And I had to make sure Shirley was all right. She's going to have her kittens any day now."

"How *is* Uncle Vic?" I asked.

Aunt Adabelle looked surprised, but she laughed. "How *is* he? He's *dead*, Shanny. But you already know that."

"Well, I can't be sure," I said. "Not when you go up there to talk with him." I was a little shocked at myself for going on with it. But I was disappointed. I had thought I had cured Aunt Adabelle of going up to the Bride's House. "If you talk with him, he must come there, too. So I just wondered how he is."

"Lands, Shanny, he doesn't come." She looked thoughtful. "Well, maybe he does. Or maybe he's just *there*."

"Is he up in the attic, too?" I asked. "I saw pictures of him up there." I tried to flip a pancake the way Aunt Adabelle did but succeeded only in plopping it on the floor, messy and half baked.

"No. He's not up there." Aunt Adabelle took the pancake turner and demonstrated how to do it, then handed it back to me.

"I'm embarrassed that you saw how I wallow around in the past up there. You must think I'm right foolish, dressing up in my old clothes and sitting there visiting with those pictures. *I should* be sorting through all that stuff and throwing most of it away."

So that's what she did up there. "It's all right, Aunt Adabelle. I just wish I could help you some way."

"Why, you have, Shanny," Aunt Adabelle said. "You've brought life to this lonely old house again. And you're here taking care of me so I can stay this last summer."

Me taking care of *her*? That was a laugh. It was the other way around.

But this time I did a perfect flip on the pancake, and it landed golden brown and light right where I wanted it.

Bucky gave me my first riding lesson on Blastoff that day. Neither Blastoff nor I were very happy about it. When I remembered that he had piled Bill Nordstrom in just three seconds twenty years before, I wasn't at all anxious to get on his back.

But Bucky insisted. "He won't hurt you," he said. "When you're all dressed up in your queen dress and all, he'll walk like a million dollars."

But that day his walk wasn't worth two cents. The fact was that he *wouldn't* walk. When Bucky put a saddle on him and led him over next to the corral rails so I could climb onto him, he just stood there, his head turned around so I could see him sneer. He refused to take a step.

"Don't worry," Bucky said. "He knows you're not the queen yet. He'll prance all over the place then."

"Bucky," I said, "how am I going to ride with a long dress? That's going to look kind of funny."

Bucky evidently hadn't considered that. But he said, "Well, what did girls do back when they wore pioneer dresses? They didn't stay off horses just because they wore long dresses, did they?"

I thought about it. "They rode sidesaddle, I guess. They had a special saddle so that they hooked one leg over a post and had both legs on the same side. That way their skirts looked nice."

"Well then," Bucky said, "just hook your leg up over the saddle horn. That way it will look like a sidesaddle."

Oh, lardy, I was going to get killed for sure if I tried something like that and the old horse actually *moved*. Experimentally I hooked one leg over the horn. It wasn't as bad as I thought. In fact, I felt kind of graceful that way.

"Okay, Bucky," I said. "I'll do it if you'll do something for me."

"What?" he said suspiciously.

"I want you to go watch 'All My Children' with Aunt Adabelle tomorrow. She's lonesome for you."

Fear clutched Bucky's face. "I'm not going to do that."

I unhooked my leg and slid off Blastoff. "Okay, then I'm not going to ride Blastoff in the parade." It was out-and-out blackmail, but I had to get things going between Bucky and Aunt Adabelle again.

Bucky looked as if he might cry. "But Blastoff's *planning* on it. He *wants* to be in the parade and carry the queen."

"Okay, then tell me why you won't go near Aunt Adabelle anymore."

"I *told* you. Because of *him*. Uncle Vic."

126

"What *about* him, Bucky? Tell me why you are so scared of him, and I promise I'll ride Blastoff."

Bucky took a deep breath and held it so long that I thought he would turn blue. Letting it out with a whoosh, he said, "It's because of the way he's—you know—dead."

"And . . . ?"

"And once last year I found a dead robin, and I put him in a cocoa can and buried him. Then this summer I dug him up and opened the can." Bucky closed his eyes and gagged.

"So you think that's the way Uncle Vic is?"

Bucky nodded. "And when she talks with him up at the Bride's House and in the attic, he must be there, and I don't want to see him. Or smell him, either." He gagged again.

I put my arm around his shoulders. "Bucky, he's not here that way. And it's not Uncle Vic she talks with in the attic." It occurred to me suddenly that I hadn't found out *who* it was she talked with in the attic. "I promise you that he's not there at the house, and especially not the way the bird was."

Bucky looked up at me. "Cross your heart?"

I crossed my heart.

He pulled away. "Okay. Tell her I'll be over to watch 'All My Children' tomorrow. I've been wondering what Erica is up to these days."

He led Blastoff over to the barn, where he took off the saddle. As I watched, I realized with a sinking heart that I was now committed to riding the old horse in the parade—if I became queen. And I would sell my Culture Club record collection to *be* queen.

We had another road-show rehearsal that night, and by the Saturday rehearsal, everybody had memorized the new parts. The mothers had worked out the choreography for their number. DeWitt and I were getting synchronized on the music, even though he still jumped every time I said anything to him. The whole show looked good.

Twyla was all over the place, spreading Nice and good cheer. "I'm so glad you came this summer, Shanny," she told me. "Thor would have been devastated if this show had gone down the drain." She was wearing her I♥ ⚡ T-shirt, the same as the rest of us.

How could I hate anybody that Nice? How could I want to snatch her guy away from her?

"That's the point," Loydene said later when we were on our way home. "That's how she's gotten everything she wanted for our whole lives. She Nices people into giving her everything she wants. You just watch. She'll Nice herself into being Pioneer Day Queen, too." Loydene sighed. "Lardy!"

I felt as if she had just punctured my tire. "Is there any use for the rest of us to even try then?"

"Oh, sure," Loydene said. "Remember, it's not over yet, Shanny. One of these days Twyla is going to O.D. on Nice, and then the rest of us will have a chance. Who knows? If we're lucky, it might be tonight."

It wasn't very Nice of me, but I hoped she was right.

Aunt Adabelle helped me dress in the completed brown gingham dress and bonnet that night. She tucked my purple tail of hair up under the bonnet and fixed the front so I had a fringe of bangs. When she let me look in the mirror, I saw a different Shanny than I had ever seen before.

"If Thor doesn't lose his heart tonight, he doesn't have eyes in his head." Aunt Adabelle twitched at the skirt and adjusted a sleeve.

He might lose his heart, all right, but I just hoped it was to *me*.

Aunt Adabelle lurched us to the square dance in the old Chevy, assuring me all the way that it was no disgrace to go to the community events without a date. "None of the other young folks will have dates," she said, "except those who are sweet on each other."

I guess she was right because they all seemed to be flying solo when we got there, except for a few like Trish Harker and R. G. Cole, who held hands as they waited for the music to start. They were, as Aunt Adabelle said, sweet on each other.

There was a big crowd at the dance, and they seemed to be all ages, from old folks to little kids. In fact, there were several babies asleep on the benches along the wall, all wrapped up in light summer blankets.

Thor wasn't there yet, but Twyla was, and when I saw her, I felt like a little gingham duck next to a beautiful swan. She had one of those old-fashioned, high-necked white dresses that are all lace and ruffles. She looked like a bride. She was smiling and laughing with everyone, but I noticed she kept looking toward the door. I knew she was watching for Thor.

When she saw me, she came right over. "Shanny," she said, "you look absolutely marvelous. The rest of us girls won't have a chance in the queen contest."

"Thanks, Twyla," I said. "But *you* don't have to worry. You look fantastic."

But Twyla wasn't listening. She was looking toward the door, and when I followed her gaze, I saw that Thor's family had arrived. After saying "Hi," Bucky went off with another boy. Mr. and Mrs. Jorgensen greeted us and continued on into the hall.

But Thor stood there looking at the two of us, his eyes going from one to the other. Even if he never said another word to me, the look on his face when he turned my way was enough to carry me through life until I was as old as Aunt Adabelle.

The band—a violin, trumpet, and piano—started tuning up, and the caller shouted, "Take your partners and form your squares."

Thor's eyes went back and forth from Twyla to me a few more times. Then he stepped forward, his hand outstretched.

13

"Hi, Twyla," Thor said, touching her on the arm as my hopes crashed in flames. He had chosen *her*.

"You look so beautiful," he said to her.

But then he turned to me. "Hi, Shanny," he said softly. "You're a real knockout."

My hopes sprang from the flames like a phoenix and shot off into the stratosphere like a launching of the Columbia space shuttle.

His hand was warm on my arm, and his eyes fried mine. He was going to ask me to be his partner for the first square, right there in front of Twyla.

But then he said, "If you girls will excuse me, I'm going to ask Aunt Adabelle for this first dance."

"What a nice idea," Twyla said. Relief was scribbled all over her face, and I knew it was because he hadn't asked *me*.

With another smile at both of us, Thor left.

"He's *so* thoughtful of Aunt Adabelle," Twyla said.

She began moving away from me, probably so that when the first set of dances was over, he would have a direct line to her without me in the way.

Before she could leave, DeWitt came sidling along, his eyes owly as he looked from Twyla to me. Maybe he intended to ask one of us to dance, or maybe he was just passing by. Twyla reached out and took his arm.

"DeWitt," she said sweetly, "they need another couple for that square over there. Let's go help them out, shall we?" She gave him a smile that cooked his face, turning it as red as the shirt he wore. "I'd really like that, Twyla," he said.

I didn't even have to look to know that the square she was dragging him toward was the one Thor and Aunt Adabelle had just joined.

Loydene had been off to one side, watching the whole scene. Now she came over to stand by me. "She's in great form tonight. Good-bye, queen contest."

I laughed. "In the immortal words of Loydene Truesdale, 'It's not over yet.' Now smile, in case one of the judges is looking our way."

We both gave our teeth an airing, and I had a chance to look Loydene over. She wore a blue calico dress, the kind you would imagine a pioneer girl wearing to a square dance back in the nineteenth century. It had a wide ruffle around the bottom of the skirt that made it flare out when she walked. There were elbow-length puffed sleeves and a dainty white collar. The blue of the bonnet kind of subdued her freckles and brought out the color of her eyes.

"You really look cute, Loydene," I said.

"Thanks." She blushed a little as if she weren't used

to compliments. "I decided to make a more simple dress than most of the girls do. Seems to me those first pioneers here in Wolf Creek wouldn't have had anything too very fancy." She looked me up and down. "You look fabulous, Shanny. That dress is just right on you."

"Thanks to you, Loydene. You picked the material."

Up on the stage, the band played a couple of chords.

"There's room for at least two more squares," the caller said. "Come on, you cowpokes, grab those purty gals and get ready to swing."

"It's hard to get the guys out there on the floor at first," Loydene told me. "I don't know why because they love it once they get going."

I felt a touch on my sleeve. I looked up to empty air, then down to see Bucky.

"Shanny," he said, "would you dance with me?"

"Sure, Bucky. I'd love to." I reached down to take his hand. "See you later, Loydene."

Bucky looked over his shoulder as we walked out on the floor. "I'd like to dance with *you* next, Loydene," he said.

"It's a date," she said.

Bucky leaned back to look behind me. "What happened to your purple hair?"

"It's tucked up under my bonnet," I said. "I didn't think it really went with the dress."

He nodded. "Maybe not."

We took our place in a square made up of Trish Harker and R. G. Cole, Dannalee Davis and a guy named Gordie something, and Perlie Truesdale and a bald-headed man whom I hadn't seen before.

"Who's your date, Bucky?" Perlie asked. "I don't believe I know this young lady."

Bucky giggled. "She's not my date. My mom won't let me have dates yet. It's Shanny, Sister Truesdale. Shanny-who's-staying-with-Aunt-Adabelle."

"Shanny?" Perlie adjusted her eyeglasses. "Lardy, I would never of knowed her." She poked the little man beside her. "That's the girl I was telling you about, Melvin."

Melvin looked me over. "She looks like a right nice little girl, Perlie. I thought you said . . . " He stopped as if he had just realized I could hear everything they said. Pumping his head up and down, he said, "A *right* nice little girl." He gave me a shy smile.

I liked Melvin.

"I would never of knowed her," Perlie said to him. "She's like a whole entire different person."

It kind of ticked me off. Was I any less of a person when I had the purple hair and the eye shadow and the Boy George T-shirt?

I didn't have much time to be mad because the other people were all welcoming Bucky and me to the square, and then the caller started yelling directions.

"First we're going to do the 'Texas Star,' " he said. "We'll walk through it first just so's everyone will remember it." Holding the microphone close to his mouth, he called, "Ladies to the center and back to the bar. Gents to the center and form a star."

I was the only one who had never square-danced before, so everyone guided me to the right place until I got the hang of it. By the time we did it to music, I knew a little about what to do. It was fun. I learned to kind of

trot around like the others and how to listen to the caller
and do what he said.

"Meet your pretty girl and pass her by. Hook the next
girl on the fly."

I found I was arm in arm with R. G. Cole, and he
was aiming his nice grin at me. Then I was being swung
around by Melvin, who really knew how to dance. We
followed directions to "promenade home" and then repeated the whole thing again. When it was over, we
were back with our original partners, all laughing and
gasping for breath as we clapped for more.

I noticed that Loydene was dancing in the next square
with U Haul, looking small alongside his big bulk. He
raised a ham-sized hand to wave when he saw me, then
pulled an enormous red handkerchief from his pocket
to mop his forehead.

There were two other dances in that set, one called
"Birdie in the Cage" and another called "Alabama Ju-
bilee."

After they were over, we had a little break so that
everyone could go to the refreshment table and have
some punch. Bucky took me there and made sure I had
a drink before he excused himself. "I promised Loydene
I'd dance with her next," he said solemnly. "Thanks for
dancing with me, Shanny. I'll see you when it's time for
the queen contest." He went off, headed for Loydene.

Across the refreshment table I saw Thor looking around
as he were searching for somebody. When he saw me,
his face lit up and he began to make his way through
the crowd.

Just then U Haul stopped by my side. "You sure look
nice, Shanny," he said. "I'm a big clumsy ox out on the

floor, but I'd sure be happy if you'd dance with me."

"I'd like to, U Haul." I didn't dare look to see if Thor was still heading my way. I didn't want to have my face tattling on my thoughts and hurting U Haul's feelings. But as we walked out out onto the floor, I noticed that Twyla had intercepted Thor.

The next dance was a Virginia reel. U Haul and I were at the head of the long line, so we were the first ones to go all the way down, swinging around with each guy or girl. After each swing with somebody else, U Haul swung me so hard that he lifted me right off my feet.

Thor did the same thing when I got to him. "If U Haul can do it, so can I," he said, laughing in my ear as he sailed me through the air. It was the first time I had been in his arms, and I wanted to stay there forever, literally swept off my feet.

But he let go of me, and I was swung by U Haul and found myself facing DeWitt. I wondered if he would run as I danced toward him.

He didn't. He took me in his arms kind of timidly and swung me in a wide circle. "Shanny, I'd sure like to have the next dance," he said.

I was flattered, thinking my beauty had stunned him out of his fear of me. Maybe he had even fallen in love with me!

"Shanny," he said urgently when the Virginia reel was over and he led me to the next set of squares, "will you tell me some of those 'did you knows?' You know, like the ones you tell us at the road-show rehearsals. I think Twyla really likes me, and I don't know what to say to her."

Well, so much for my stunning beauty.

"Okay, DeWitt." I thought fast. It was almost time for us to do-si-do and grand-right-and-left. "Did you know there is a town named Kissimmee, Florida?"

DeWitt flushed. "Oh, I wouldn't dare say that to Twyla."

I thought fast again. I wished I had read up on more facts. There had been so much going on recently that I hadn't even had time to open up *The People's Almanac* or a *National Geographic*. "Well, did you know there's a town named Monkey's Eyebrow, Kentucky?"

"Oh, that's good," DeWitt said. "She'll laugh at that one. Do you have any more?"

"Swing your partner and do-si-do," the caller yelled. "Right and left, around we go."

"Did you know," I said as we swung around, "that it takes ten years for the eggs of a water flea to hatch?"

"Oh, thanks, Shanny," DeWitt breathed as we sashayed around one another.

When our set was over, DeWitt, armed with his new facts, went off in search of Twyla, and miracle of miracles, Thor suddenly appeared at my side.

"I thought I'd never catch you between guys," he said. "May I have the next dance, Shanny?"

It was something called "The Blackhawk Waltz," but it should have been "I Could Have Danced All Night" from *My Fair Lady* because that's the way I felt as he held me close.

The queen contest took place during intermission. A woman got up and announced that all the girls who were participating should form a circle and walk around the hall so the judges could take a look at their costumes.

After we did that, each girl was supposed to go up on stage and be introduced by Mr. Jorgensen, Thor's father, who was the master of ceremonies. Then we were all supposed to stay up there until the winner was announced.

At that point I wasn't sure if I would last the night. My legs were trembling from all the dancing, or maybe it was from nervousness about the contest. Or it could have been I was just weak from the experience of being in Thor's arms for a whole dance.

Each girl could say something if she wanted to while she was on the stage. Most of them just said something about how much fun they were having. Twyla made a little speech about how nice it was that we had a Pioneer Day celebration to honor those first settlers, and Loydene made everybody laugh when she said it was all right to wear our long skirts to a dance, but she was glad she didn't have to wear one out to the barn to milk the cows.

When it was my turn to go up there, everybody yelled out for me to "Give us a fact, Shanny."

I couldn't think of any more facts. If I told the same ones I had given DeWitt, Twyla would know for sure that they came from me, and she might be mad at him.

What facts hadn't I already told them?

"Give us a fact, give us a fact, give us a fact." Kids were chanting like cheerleaders at a football game.

A fact. Desperately I fished around in my brain. "Did you know . . ." I could remember only one—the one Flame had once told at another party. "Did you know," I said, "that when the ancient Egyptians made a mummy, they injected something like turpentine into the abdomen to dissolve the guts?"

I knew I had lost the queen contest before the words were out of my mouth—before I saw the shocked look on Perlie Truesdale's face and before Twyla came up and put her arm around my shoulders and said, "Isn't Shanny full of the most interesting facts?" Before she accidentally brushed my bonnet off so that everybody could see my jagged hair and that purple tail and know how freaky I really was.

I didn't even want to stay for the announcement of the queen, but Loydene took hold of my hand and kept me there.

I felt I had let Bucky down. Blastoff, old snob that he was, wouldn't want to carry me in the parade if I wasn't the queen.

And I would never follow in my mom's footsteps and have Thor fall in love with me as I rode in the parade.

After the introductions there was some time while the judges tabulated their opinions. My heart thudded in my chest just like Blastoff's heavy feet during one of his midnight performances in the corral.

Then Mr. Jorgensen went to the microphone again. "As you know, this has been a very difficult decision. Any one of these young women would do our town honor as queen. But here is the judges' decision. They have picked a queen and two attendants." He consulted the paper in his hand. "The second attendant is Dot Myers."

The girl named Dot, looking only a little bit disappointed, walked to the center of the stage while everybody cheered.

"The first attendant," said Mr. Jorgensen, "is Dannalee Davis."

Dannalee, in a peach-colored dress, walked over to join Dot.

Twyla's smile lit up the stage as she waited for her name to be announced.

"Lardy," Loydene whispered in my ear, "it's going to be *you*."

Mr. Jorgensen cleared his throat. "The judges say they picked the queen because she looks the way they figure a Wolf Creek girl of one hundred years ago would look. The queen of this year's Wolf Creek Pioneer Day celebration and rodeo is none other than *Loydene Truesdale*."

Loydene! I turned to give her a great big delighted hug.

"Me?" Loydene said. She looked a little bewildered. "Me? Did he say me?"

"He sure did, Loydene," I told her. "Now go over there and take your bows."

"Lardy," she whispered, "I can't believe it." Then she straightened her back and walked like a queen to the center of the stage to accept the applause of the crowd.

The light that was Twyla's smile had gone out. She joined the rest of us who hadn't made it as we went down off the stage.

DeWitt met her at the bottom of the stairs. "I thought it would be you," he said. "I really did, Twyla."

She didn't look at him.

DeWitt followed her. "I'd sure be happy if you'd dance the next set with me."

Twyla pushed her way through the crowd, headed for the door.

"Twyla," DeWitt said, "listen to this." He put a hand on her arm, holding her back. "Did you know that there's a town in Kentucky named Monkey's Eyebrow?"

She yanked her arm away from his hand. "Monkey's Eyebrow yourself, DeWitt," she said. "Bug off and leave me alone."

Twyla's Nice had cracked, just the way Loydene had predicted it might. But it had shattered all over DeWitt, and I couldn't be happy about it at all.

14

Twyla didn't come to church the next day, but DeWitt did. The eager DeWitt of the night before was gone, though, and he was back to looking owly and scared. I wanted to go up and pat him on the head and say, "There, there, it will be all right," the way Mom used to do when I skinned a knee or bumped my head. I was ashamed that I had ever thought he was just a wimp. Maybe it's not until we see another person bleed that we realize he or she is a real live human being who hurts when hacked.

DeWitt played the organ for the church services, and when they were over, he slid off the bench and headed for the door. I guess other people also felt kind of protective because I saw U Haul clap him on the back as he went by, and Trish Harker and R. G. Cole said something that made him smile. Others reached out to him, and by the time he got to where Loydene and I were standing, I wasn't sure he even needed my little contribution.

But I said it anyway. "Hi, DeWitt. Did you know that you're just as great on the organ as you are on the synthesizer?"

I thought he might edge past me because I was in my weird clothes again, but he stopped and cleared his throat. "Did you know that the embalmed body of Charlemagne sat on his throne for 400 years after his death?" He smiled shyly. "I just read that this morning."

"That's really good, DeWitt," I said. "Do you mind if I write it to my friend in California?"

DeWitt's face glowed red. "That's okay, Shanny. I hope she likes it." Ducking his head, he hurried away.

Loydene watched him go. "That was nice, Shanny. You made him feel good."

We started to move out of the chapel. People stopped Loydene to tell her how happy they were that she had won the title of Pioneer Day Queen. She smiled and thanked each one.

When we got outside, I said, "Speaking of Nice, I wonder where Twyla is today."

Loydene gazed at the dark clouds that hung over the blue mountains in the distance down in the valley toward Pratt. "She's probably home sulking. Lardy, I almost feel sorry for her. This is the first time her Nice hasn't gotten her what she wanted. I don't think she knows how to handle it. I guess it was too much for her to lose the queen contest and Thor, too, all in the same night."

"What do you mean, lose Thor?"

"Well, not that she ever *had* him," Loydene said. "I mean, I think she just kept Nicing him into situations

143

where he felt he had to ask her out or hurt her feelings."

She hadn't answered my question. "Loydene, what do you mean she 'lost' him? Is Thor dropping her because of what she did to DeWitt?"

Loydene looked at me. "Lardy, Shanny, don't be dense. I saw how he looked at you when you were dancing together last night."

I'd swear my heart stopped beating and just sat quivering in my chest. "Me? You think Thor likes *me*?"

Loydene laughed. "You sound just like I did when they announced I am the queen. Of course Thor likes you, you nerd. Anybody with a pair of eyes could see that he was looking at you last night as if you were the world's largest lemon meringue pie. Which, I might give you a hint, is his favorite dessert."

I hardly heard her. I was trying to process the information that *Thor liked me*. It wouldn't process. It kept hitting such barriers as: *Why* does he like me? That is, if he *does* like me. Does he feel sorry for me? Does he think I'm so pathetic that he wants to improve my self-image, the way he wanted to improve that of all the kids in Wolf Creek?

It almost blew out my circuits. I mean, it was what I had hoped for ever since I came to Wolf Creek, but the reality was more than I could handle. If it *was* reality.

"He hasn't said more than hello to me today, Loydene," I told her. "That doesn't sound to me like a guy who's drooling over the world's largest lemon meringue pie."

"He and U Haul are fussing around about road-show

scenery this morning," Loydene said. "Give him time."

She said she would call me that afternoon about four o'clock about getting together so I could show her how the Rose Queen waved to the crowd as she rode her float through the streets of Pasadena in the Tournament of Roses parade.

"I want to do it right," she said.

That's why I thought it was Loydene calling that afternoon when the telephone rang a few minutes before four.

I picked up the receiver. "Shanny's Pie House," I said. "The lemon meringue pie speaking."

There was a short silence, then a male voice said, "How did you know that's just what I wanted?"

Thor!

I almost said it was a wrong number and hung up. I mean, aside from everything else, he was going to think I had been *asking* about what kind of food he liked. It too much of a coincidence for me to have just picked lemon meringue pie out of the blue.

"Shanny?" Thor said. "Are you there?"

"I'm here," I admitted.

"I was just wondering if you're tied up with anything right now."

He spoke as if I might possibly be having the President of the United States to tea or something. I couldn't very well say I had been sitting there thinking about him, so I said, "I was writing a letter to Flame." Which wasn't really a lie because I had my stationery there and had thought about writing a letter.

"I was just thinking I'd take you on that tour of Wolf Creek I promised you a couple of weeks ago. If you don't mind seeing it in the rain, that is. I think it's going to start to pour pretty soon."

"I'll bring my umbrella," I said.

Thor's truck was cozy as we drove up and down the hills of Wolf Creek. It hardly ever rains in southern California, and I loved the sound of the drops on the roof of the truck. They made a kind of drum-beat background for Thor's guided tour.

He took me first a little way into the national forest that bordered Wolf Creek on the north, where we had a drink of icy cold water from a pipe that came directly from a spring in the ground.

"Strawberry Springs water is the best in the world," he told me, and I believed him. I had never tasted water that wasn't full of chlorine before.

He showed me a steep little road that led along a ridge and down to the river, where he said the kids had swimming parties in the summertime. "We'll go there one night right after the road shows are over," he told me. That was something to look forward to.

When he showed me the ball park on the banks of Wolf Creek, he said that was where the parade and rodeo would be the following Saturday. "By the way," he said, "Bucky still wants you to ride old Blastoff. He says Blastoff won't mind carrying the prettiest girl in town even if she isn't the queen."

I could feel myself blushing a little. "I guess I'll have to do that for my No. 1 fan."

"Is Bucky your No. 1 fan, Shanny?" Thor asked. "I thought I was."

We were driving now along an unpaved road that led up to where Thor said there had once been a haunted house. Tall trees overhung the road, and when Thor looked over at me, I thought I must have been transported into some romantic movie. When he pulled over to the side of the road and stopped, I knew he was going to draw me gently to his chest and murmur, "Oh, Shanny, I've wanted to do this for such a long time." And then he would kiss me.

I was trying to decide whether or not I was ready for it when he leaned out of the window and yelled, "Hey, U Haul. Come here. I think I've figured out what to do about that scenery problem."

When I peered through the rain in front of the truck, I saw that U Haul was coming along the narrow road on a horse. He rode over and greeted us; then he and Thor talked about their scenery problem while the horse snorted and I cooled off from my overheated romantic dreams.

We didn't finish our tour. The rain began coming down even harder. U Haul said he was getting too wet from the rain, so he rode off, and Thor said we'd better go back to Aunt Adabelle's to see that the windows of the henhouse were closed and that Blastoff had been put inside the barn.

"Bucky's probably taken care of everything," Thor said. "But we'd better check, anyway."

Bucky wasn't around when we got back to the ranch. Neither was Aunt Adabelle, although the henhouse windows were closed and Blastoff was snug in the barn.

"They might be up at the Bride's House," I said. "Aunt

Adabelle's been going up there again to talk with Uncle Vic. And Bucky's been worried about Shirley. He says it's time for her to have her kittens."

"We'd better go up there," Thor said. "This rain is so heavy that I wouldn't want Aunt Adabelle trying to make it back down the mountain alone."

I found some umbrellas and a flashlight, and we started up the steep path. The rain was making new little gullies in the dirt, and we slipped and slid as we climbed.

"Have you found out what Aunt Adabelle talks about with Uncle Vic?" Thor asked.

I tried to remember what she had said the day we talked about it. "She's worried about leaving the ranch, I think," I said. "She talks that over with him. She talks to somebody in the attic, too, but I don't know who that is."

"I'm sorry you've had to deal with this all alone, Shanny," Thor said. "I should have come over to help you with it, but I've been so busy with that road show that I've kind of let everything else slide."

"It's okay," I said. "I don't know whether or not you could have done anything anyway. She's not dangerous or anything like that."

"You don't think she might get it into her head that he wants her to come with him, do you?" Thor asked. "I mean, if she's so worried about leaving, she might . . . you know."

I hadn't even thought about anything like that. Certainly Aunt Adabelle had never given me any indication that she was suicidal.

"Oh, Thor, we'd better hurry," I said, puffing.

When we got a little closer, we saw that there was a dim light in the Bride's House.

"She's lit the kerosene lamp," Thor said. "There's smoke coming from the chimney, so she's built a fire in the stove."

Like a stage set, I thought, a stage set for some kind of drama. We hurried faster.

I'm not sure just what we expected to see when we burst through the door of the Bride's House, but it certainly wasn't what we did see. Aunt Adabelle and Bucky were crouched on the rag rug in front of the old stove, and Shirley was between them. A kitten was in the process of being born.

Both Aunt Adabelle and Bucky looked up when we came in.

"I'm sure glad you came," Aunt Adabelle said. "Shirley's having real trouble with this kitten."

The cat was making little mrrr mrrr sounds as she licked at herself. As we came closer, we saw that one tiny paw was sticking out of her.

"It's turned wrong," Aunt Adabelle said. "She won't let me touch her."

Thor dropped to his knees beside the straining cat. She looked at him, startled. For a moment I thought she was going to run away.

"It's okay, Shirley," Bucky murmured, petting her head. She let him touch her, but she hissed when Thor put out his hand.

I watched, fascinated. I had never seen anything born before.

"It's like when Rosie had her calf," Bucky said. "Its

leg came out first, and Dad had to reach in and turn it around so it could come out the right way. But a cat's too little to do that."

I realized this was nothing new for Bucky, and certainly not for Aunt Adabelle and Thor. They were all considering what would be the best thing to do. I felt useless, so I just stood where I was, watching.

"Bucky," Thor said, "you keep petting her. Try to keep her from biting me. I'm going to see what I can do."

Bucky gently took Shirley's head between his two hands, leaning close to murmur to her. Aunt Adabelle reached out and held the cat's sharp-clawed front feet.

There was one thing I could do to help. I shifted the old kerosene lamp to the edge of the table where its soft light would be more useful, and I turned on the flashlight I had in my hand, aiming it at the delivery scene.

"Thanks, Shanny," Thor said. He was trying to poke the one little paw back inside the cat, but she was struggling and trying to bite him.

"Shirley," Bucky whispered anxiously. "You have to let him do it. He's trying to help you."

The cat hissed.

"I think it's her first litter," Aunt Adabelle said. "She's frightened."

Thor stroked Shirley's side. "It's going to be all right, old girl. Just take it easy." Pressing her abdomen with his fingers, he said, "I think maybe I can shift the others back so that first one will have some room. But you'll have to hang on to her."

The others bent closer to the cat.

The thing that impressed me was how much they *cared*.

Shirley was just an abandoned stray, but they cared about her and the babies she was trying to produce. They cared about so many things, these three. Where had I missed out on the caring? It wasn't that Mom and Dad didn't care. They were always doing nice things for people. And for me. And what about other people where I lived? There was Mrs. Midgely who took in stray dogs and found homes for them. And the Joneses who always had two or three foreign students living with them, and old Mr. Hines who was always going out to sweep up the leaves and trash that the garbage men and the street sweeper missed. I could think of dozens of people who *cared*. Where had *I* been? All huddled up deep inside myself, that's where I'd been. Worrying about how I couldn't compete with the beauty queens and the super achievers. Worrying about the lifeguard with the dragon tattoed on his chest. Worrying about all the things that didn't matter and not taking time to even look at those that did. Wasn't caring as important as being a beauty queen or a whiz kid?

"I think it's coming," Thor said tensely. "Yes. Look, here's No. 1."

While I had been wandering around in my head, Thor had gotten the kitten turned so that it could be born. Now it lay quietly on the rug while Shirley licked it.

"It's not breathing," Bucky said.

Thor touched it. "Maybe we've lost this one. But there are others, Bucky. I'd say she's going to have at least two more."

Bucky looked at him, urgency on his face. "But it tried so hard to be born. It wants to live, too."

Suddenly I cared as much as he did about the limp

151

little kitten that wasn't responding to its mother's licking.

"Here, hold this," I said to Bucky, handing him the flashlight. I had hated the first-aid classes we had had in school. I hadn't cared to learn how to help someone else, but I had learned a few things in spite of myself.

I picked up the tiny, slimy kitten. Shirley didn't make objection because she was working on the second one.

Prying the kitten's mouth open, I blew into it. Then I touched its fragile rib cage, pushing it very gently. I repeated the process several times. It still didn't breathe. In desperation I took its head with one hand and its back part with the other and folded them gently together so that its head was in the crotch of its back legs. I repeated that several times, too.

Suddenly the kitten twitched and gasped. It gave a weak mew. Then it began to breathe.

I couldn't believe it. But there it was, lying in my hands, feebly moving its head and legs.

"Oh, Shanny," Bucky said. "It's alive!"

It *was* alive because of what I had done for it. *I* had made the difference.

I couldn't say anything to Bucky because my throat was all choked up. This is what it's all about, I thought. This is why Thor works so hard to make his road show a success. This is why Aunt Adabelle has had so many young people in her home. This is why Bucky is so anxious to restore Blastoff to his former glory at the rodeo, if only for one day. They want to make a difference.

"I'm going to name that kitten Shanny," Bucky said,

and I felt as honored as if somebody had built a monument for me in the center of Washington, D.C.

Shirley had three kittens in all. Shanny was the smallest, and the only female. The other two were big strong males. But little Shanny was my favorite, and I was already worried about what was going to happen to her.

"What are you going to do with Shirley and her kittens?" I asked.

Aunt Adabelle smiled. She was sitting in the old rocker by the stove now, and the soft lamplight made her look younger than she was. "Why, we'll let them all stay here, I guess," she said. "Shirley seems to like it here, and she has been keeping the mouse population down."

"I'll take care of them," Bucky said. "I just love kittens."

"We'll put you in charge," Aunt Adabelle said. I knew she was thinking of the time when she'd be leaving the ranch.

Thor grinned. "I'll be in charge of taking Shirley to Dr. Barlow in Pratt to be spayed as soon as the kittens are weaned. Later on I'll take the kittens in, too. We don't want to overdo this blessed event."

"Looks like that's one thing I won't have to worry about, doesn't it, Vic?" Aunt Adabelle said.

Bucky, who was lying on the floor admiring the kittens, looked up, his eyes huge. "Is *he* here?" he asked.

Aunt Adabelle chuckled as she rocked. "No, he's not here. It's just that this is where we began our life together. We were young, then, and full of dreams and anything seemed possible. Now that I'm old and confused and things are changing so fast, I like to come here and remember. It's a place of love, Bucky, and I feel as if I can get in touch with him here." She looked over at me and Thor and added, "We were married almost sixty years, Vic and I. After that long you get to be part of one another."

Thor and I were sitting on the little day bed that stood against one wall. The rain was still beating against the windowpanes, and occasionally there was even a flash of lightning. Shirley was asleep on the rug by the stove, her three new babies warm against her. The fire in the old stove crackled softly, and the lamplight flickered, making friendly shadows on the walls.

It *was* a place of love, and as Thor reached over and took my hand, I, too, believed that anything was possible. Thor's road show was going to be a winner. Blast-off was going to have a really good day at the rodeo. Something would happen so Aunt Adabelle could stay on at the ranch. And Thor was going to fall in love with me, and we were going to be happy together for sixty years or more.

I wished later that we had all just stayed there in that cozy, safe little house.

15

Bucky gave me a couple more riding lessons during the week. There was plenty of time for them because Aunt Adabelle still wasn't doing any packing, and Thor had told me he was going to be really busy this last week before the road shows were presented. I interpreted that as meaning that he wouldn't be around to see me much that week but that I had a lot to look forward to after the shows were over.

Actually, the riding lessons turned out to be more like sitting lessons. All I did was sit on Blastoff's back while he sneered and gave big gusty sighs to show how bored he was with it all. He wouldn't budge an inch while I sat on him, and Bucky had to lead him around so I could get used to his movements. Bucky swore that it would make all the difference in the world when Blastoff saw a crowd watching him.

"He'll parade around then as proud as you please," he said.

I was a little nervous. "Don't you think he might start bucking?" I asked from my high perch on Blastoff's back.

"Well, see," Bucky said, "when you want a horse to buck, you put a flank cinch on him, and that makes him mad and he bucks to try to get rid of it. He won't buck without a flank cinch."

"You're sure, Bucky?" I didn't like the way Blastoff's ears were laid back against his head.

"*Pretty* sure," Bucky said.

That didn't improve my confidence much. But it meant so much to Bucky that I decided I had to go through with it. Besides, since I wasn't the queen, I wasn't going to wear a dress, so I wouldn't have to ride sidesaddle, and that made it not quite so scary.

What I was going to wear was Loydene's fawn-colored western riding outfit, which really looked nice on me. To tell the truth, I was sort of looking forward to the parade.

We had road-show rehearsals every night that week. Thor was so excited about the way it was going that he was making up "Did you knows" all over the place.

"Did you know," he said to the cast one night, "that they're going to have to create a special category just to rate us?"

"Are we that bad?" U Haul asked.

"We're that *good*," Thor said. "But don't get big heads about it or we're likely to fall flat on our faces. We could still fail, you know."

Just to prove he was wrong, we did the next run-through even better than the last.

DeWitt and I were working well together now. I knew

what to expect from him, and I wove my drumming in around his music so that we really had a good sound. I had worked out some neat drum rolls at the end of some of the songs, and I had a catchy rhythm for the tap dancers that helped make their number the hit of the show.

By the night of the dress rehearsal, we were all sure we would go right on to perform in Hollywood—or at least in Pratt.

Twyla had been coming to rehearsals all week, but she wasn't making any effort to be super Nice anymore. She wasn't nasty or anything like that, but she wasn't gushing all over the place, either. She just came and did her part, which was to stand in one of the compartments in the Rent-A-Rama scenery that she had designed and model a gorgeous dress. When the storekeeper tried to sell costumes to the girls, Twyla stepped out and twirled around a couple of times. In her flounced yellow dress she was enough to make even DeWitt, who was still pretty upset over her, lose his place in the music and bring the whole show to a stop.

Watching her, I got discouraged again, but then I had to make up my mind not to worry about her anymore. There were always going to be girls more beautiful than I, wherever I went. That didn't mean *all* the good things were going to happen to *them*, did it? I had to keep reminding myself of that because Thor was really nice to her, as always, so I also had to keep reminding myself that that's the way Thor was.

I wrote a letter to Flame after the Friday night rehearsal. I made it like a soap opera, telling her everything that had been happening and ending up with: "Will

Shanny ever find real happiness? Will Shanny ever find the real Shanny? Will Blastoff blast off? For the answers to these and other earthshaking questions, tune in to my next letter."

Saturday arrived, hot and clear. I got up early to help Bucky curry Blastoff, as I had promised. We were supposed to be at the ball park by 10:30 because the parade was going to start at 11:00. After that everyone would have a picnic and visit with one another; then the amateur rodeo would start at 1:00, so there would be plenty of time afterward to go home and rest and do the evening chores. Everyone who was in the road show was supposed to be at the church at 6:00 P.M. for make-up, and the shows were to start at 7:30.

Bucky was already at the corral when I got there. "Blastoff knows this is the big day," he said. "He's been watching for you."

When I looked at him, Blastoff seemed to be watching the inside of his eyelids, but I took Bucky's word for it.

We took him into the barn, where Bucky fed him some hay, adding a heaping side dish of oats because of the special occasion. Blastoff munched away while we ran the curry combs over his body, pulling out any dried dirt and matted hair. His hide rippled as we worked, and he seemed to be enjoying it.

Bucky combed out his fetlocks and polished his hooves while I tried to make his stringy mane look presentable.

I had an idea. "Bucky, would you like me to braid some ribbons into his mane? That would really dress him up."

Bucky's eyes shone. "Oh, yes, he'd like that." He patted the old horse's neck. "That will make everybody look at him, and he just loves to show off."

I ran back to the house, where Aunt Adabelle stirred around and found some long red ribbons that had once been belts for matching dresses she had made for Mom and The Cousins.

"Go ahead and cut them up," she said. "Anything you can use makes that much less stuff we have to get rid of."

I couldn't see that Aunt Adabelle had gotten rid of anything so far, but at least I understood why it was so hard for her now. I wondered what Mom and Dad would say if I wrote to them and said I wanted to stay there on the ranch with Aunt Adabelle. I could take care of her so she wouldn't have to leave, and also be there for my future with Thor. I only had about ten days left there, and I couldn't stand to think of leaving him.

I would have to think about that later because we had to get Blastoff ready for the parade.

When I got back to the barn, I cut the ribbons in the right lengths to braid into Blastoff's mane and forelock and even braided a couple into his tail. It almost spaced Bucky out.

"He looks *glorious*," he said, standing back to admire Blastoff. "He'll be the best-looking horse in the whole parade."

Glorious Blastoff switched his beribboned tail, closed his eyes, and gave a bored sigh.

Bucky's father came with his horse trailer to haul Blastoff the two miles to the ball park because Bucky was afraid it would tire him out to walk that far. After they left, Aunt Adabelle and I got ready, and she drove us to the green ball park on the banks of Wolf Creek.

I was surprised at how many people were there, but Aunt Adabelle told me they came from all over the county to take part in the celebration. There was only one section of bleachers, but people were sitting under the trees by the creek, and others had front-row seats next to the slat fence that had been put up to form an arena.

I found Bucky and Blastoff in an adjoining field, where the parade participants were gathering. Thor was there, too, with U Haul, and they seemed to be doing something to get everybody organized. Thor waved to me, but he didn't come over to speak.

"Loydene wants to see you," Bucky said. He pointed up toward the front of the parade.

On my way there I passed a bunch of people on horses whose shirts said, "Ranch Riders of Wolf Creek." There was a big group of little kids dressed in pioneer costumes and some older folks pushing handcarts. There seemed to be at least a dozen floats. It was a bigger parade than I'd expected.

I found Loydene sitting alone on her covered-wagon float, looking pale and pretty. The float was just a hay wagon with a canvas cover that was pulled by a car, but it was nice.

"Lardy, Shanny," Loydene said, "am I glad to see you."

"Is something wrong?" I asked. Loydene seemed nervous.

"Look at Twyla," she said.

I looked the way she pointed and saw Twyla dressed in some kind of flowing white robes, holding something gold colored in her hand. She was standing on a chariot-like thing, which was pulled by a white horse.

"She's the Statue of Liberty, and she's going to lead the parade," Loydene said. "That's some kind of tiki torch she's got in her hand, and it's actually going to be lighted."

"Good old Twyla," I said. "How did she manage that?"

"Her dad's in charge of the parade," Loydene said glumly. "Who's going to look at me when *she's* there to look at?"

I patted Loydene's hand. "Loydene, this is *your* day. Next year and other years after that, when somebody talks about this parade, they're going to say, 'Oh, yeah, that's the parade where Loydene was the queen.' Who's going to remember who the Statue of Liberty was? *You* are the *queen*, Loydene. Twyla can't change that no matter how hard she tries. So just forget her and enjoy being this year's queen of the Wolf Creek Pioneer Day celebration."

I couldn't believe this. *I* was giving advice. I wondered where along the line I had picked up the confidence to be able to say what I was saying with such conviction. Maybe people like my mom weren't born able to hand out advice. Maybe they learned it along the way, a little at a time. Maybe other things happened a little at a time, too, like becoming a worthwhile person. Or like a marriage that was so good that Aunt Adabelle could feel close to Uncle Vic even after he was dead.

Loydene was looking ahead to Twyla's chariot. "But she's so beautiful, Shanny. Just look at her."

"So there are a lot of beautiful people in the world,

but that doesn't mean the rest of us have to stick our heads in the sand. Lardy, Loydene, *you* won the queen contest."

She giggled. "And you won Thor, Shanny."

I wasn't too sure of that, but I grinned at Loydene.

Somebody announced over the loudspeaker that all parade participants should get ready to move, so I gave Loydene a quick peck on the cheek as her attendants, Dot and Dannalee, came running over to climb on the float. Then I hurried back to Bucky and Blastoff.

The parade marched to the music of the United States Marine Band, played from a tape through some big speakers mounted on a high stand by the rodeo arena. U Haul, riding his horse and wearing a fringed buckskin jacket, led the parade, carrying the flag, which rippled in the slight breeze. Twyla's chariot was close behind him. Next there was an old-fashioned surrey, driven by R. G. Cole with Trish Harker by his side on the seat. Loydene's queen float was next. She could have been Miss America herself, the way she smiled and waved as she rode along.

Blastoff and I were right at the end because we were supposed to be the transition from the pioneer theme to the rodeo. It was a good thing we were because otherwise we would have held up the whole line. Blastoff refused to move.

"I'll lead him until we get to the arena," Bucky said.

We weren't supposed to be a comedy act, but that's what we turned out to be. Somebody spotted balky old Blastoff being towed along by Bucky, with me clinging to the saddle horn and trying to look as if I were enjoying it. They pointed fingers and started laughing. Pretty soon everybody was laughing. I don't think they meant to be unkind, but we did look ridiculous. At least I felt that way.

"Maybe we should just go ahead and play it funny," I said to Bucky when it was our turn to enter the arena and go all the way around it. Blastoff still wouldn't move on his own, and Bucky was red-faced and sweaty from pulling him along.

But Blastoff didn't want to play it funny. The laughter seemed to confuse him. I guess he was used to applause. He swung his big head from side to side, peering at the crowd. Then he tried to back out of the arena, pulling Bucky along with him. The front of the parade was arriving back at the entrance after making a full circle of the arena, and Blastoff was backing right toward Twyla's chariot.

"Whoa, Blastoff," I said. "Stop!"

U Haul rode over to see what he could do, but he was holding the flag steady with one hand and guiding his horse with the other, so he couldn't do much. Blastoff continued to back up until his rear end bumped the wheel of Twyla's cnariot, making the white horse nervous. It began to dance around. The Statue of Liberty decided to abandon ship. She leaped from her pedestal and sped out of the arena, her robes flapping behind her and her torch still flaming.

The crowd loved it. They clapped and laughed.

Bucky was almost in tears. "They're making fun of him," he said. "Tell them to stop."

Thor appeared from somewhere. "Thor," I said desperately, "you've got to ride him. He knows I'm not like the cowboys he used to carry. But if *you* get on him, maybe he'll think it's like the old days."

Bucky's face filled with hope. "Oh, Thor, would you? Please?"

"Let's just get him out of here," Thor said. He tugged at Blastoff's bridle. "He's messing up the whole parade."

"Thor," I whispered, "this means so much to Bucky. Couldn't you just ride him around the arena a couple of times?"

Thor looked at Bucky's pleading face. "Okay. Here, I'll help you down."

I wasn't sorry to get off that old horse and feel the firm earth under my feet again. I patted Blastoff's neck while Thor put his foot in the stirrup and leaped aboard.

Blastoff's expression changed as soon as he felt Thor's weight hit his back. You could almost see his brain telling him that here was someone worth considering. Here was his old enemy the cowboy. This *was* like old times.

"Give me the reins, Bucky," Thor said.

Bucky handed them up to him, and Thor pressed his heels to Blastoff's sides. The old horse trotted docilely out into the middle of the arena. The crowd's laughter changed to cheers as he flung up his head and gave them a magnificent sneer. Thor waved and grinned.

Right about then Blastoff erupted. He leaped into the air facing north and came down facing south. Thor looked startled, and Bucky screamed, "Wow, look at him go."

Blastoff became a tornado. He arched his back and kicked out his rear legs. Twisting his backbone, he sashayed sideways, snorting fearsomely as he made a stiff-legged circuit of the arena. The float participants who were still there began to leave in whatever way they could.

Blastoff stopped for a breather, peering back at Thor, who sat gamely on his back. The crowd was on its feet now, cheering like crazy. U Haul had given the flag to somebody and was riding out to rescue Thor.

Blastoff saw him coming. His eyes narrowed and his flabby lips grimaced. Then he went into a tight spin, hammerhead lowered, back bent upward, and front legs spread apart. Thor stood out parallel to the ground.

"Thor," I wailed. Oh, why had I begged him to get on that old rattlebones?

Blastoff was in his glory. Dust swirled up from his stomping feet, and the crowd was out of its mind with excitement.

I don't know just when Thor went off, but suddenly he wasn't in the saddle anymore. Blastoff had maintained his record and bucked off one more cowboy.

"Thor!" I screamed, trying to see through the thick dust while Blastoff, his head high and the red ribbons streaming from his mane and tail, made a thundering tour of the arena, sneering happily at the cheering crowd. They didn't seemed worried about Thor. I guess they were used to seeing people get bucked off horses.

Thor was trying to get up when I got to him. Some of my first-aid training came back to me. "Stay down," I said. "You might be hurt."

"I'm all right," Thor said. But then he groaned. "Well, maybe I'll just lie here for a minute."

"Better do that, buddy," U Haul said, sliding from his horse and kneeling beside Thor.

Thor groaned again. "I guess I've hurt my back. I didn't think that old plug still had it in him to pile me."

A man came running toward us with a black medical bag in his hand. "Good thing I decided to come today," he said. "That was quite a ride, son. Now let's take a look at the damages."

Thor grinned shakily at him. "Hi, Dr. Caldwell. Thought I'd seen the last of you when my arm healed."

Dr. Caldwell sighed. "Don't know how come I was so careful about delivering you young bucks. You've all been determined to bust yourselves up ever since."

"It was my fault," I said.

"Doesn't matter whose fault it was," the doctor said. "It's my job to patch up whatever's ruined." He started running his hands over Thor's legs. "Step back now, Miss. You're just in the way."

After examining him, Dr. Caldwell said he didn't think Thor had any broken bones, but he wasn't sure what was making him hurt when he tried to stand up. He decided to take him to Pratt and do some X rays.

"I can't go to Pratt," Thor said. "I've got some things to do for the road show before tonight."

"Get somebody else to do them, son," Dr. Caldwell said. "You might not even make it to the road shows."

I was too wiped out to stay for the rodeo. It was my fault that Thor was hurt. If he couldn't come to the road shows, that was my fault, too. He would probably never want to speak to me again.

Aunt Adabelle took me home, where I went upstairs and threw myself on my bed. I wished desperately that I could back up time and replay the scene at the ball park. This time I would have Blastoff buck *me* off. I

wouldn't care how much I got hurt. Who needed *me?*
The road show could go on without me and my drums,
but how could it go on without Thor? How could *I* go
on without Thor?

On the bedside table I saw the dumb notebook where
I had written "Things I Have Learned About Myself."
I grabbed the notebook and ripped the page out, crum-
pling it up and throwing it across the room.

I knew who I was. It wasn't hard to figure out. I was
the girl who was in the way, the one who always did
everything wrong.

I was a complete, absolute, total, and unreformable
dud.

16

Mrs. Jorgensen called me in the late afternoon to tell me that Thor had no broken bones but that he did have some strained ligaments.

"He'll be in bed for a few days," she said. "He can't go to the road shows tonight, which is driving him crazy. He says to tell you that it's up to you to see that our kids do a good job, Shanny."

Well, that was only right. It was my fault he couldn't go, so he was making me responsible for whatever happened to the show. I wondered if he would ever forgive me if the whole thing fell apart because he wasn't there. But how was *I* going to keep it from falling apart?

"Mrs. Jorgensen," I said, "may I speak to Thor?"

"He's asleep now, Shanny. The doctor gave him a sedative. For the pain, you know."

I felt like crying. "Mrs. Jorgensen," I said, "I'm really sorry he got hurt."

"I am, too, Shanny. But he'll be all right in a week or

so." Mrs. Jorgensen sounded as if she had been through this kind of thing before. "He wants to talk to you tomorrow."

I wasn't sure I could face him, especially if the show flopped, but I said, "I'll come over first thing in the morning."

"Fine, Shanny. The rest of us will be at the shows tonight since I'm in the Mothers' chorus and all, but he'll want to hear all about it from you. By the way, Bucky is the happiest kid alive. He's sorry that his brother is hurt, of course, but he says Blastoff is just like his old self since he bucked Thor off."

I was glad *something* good had come out of the whole thing.

I don't remember a whole lot about the road show. Everything was in a shambles when I got there at a little after 6:00 P.M. Our whole cast was gathered in our assigned make-up room, and Trish Harker was trying to pull everyone together with the help of some of the mothers. They all looked relieved when I came in, which just made me realize how much they depended on Thor.

"Here's our show biz specialist," Trish said. "She'll tell us what to do."

"Hasn't she done enough already?" Twyla said. "How can we even go on without Thor to direct the music? And what about the lines he says to the girls right in the beginning?"

Forty pairs of eyes turned toward me. A few were hostile, but most were full of hope. They were looking to *me* for help. Me, the dud of the world. What a laugh!

But as I looked back into those faces, something happened to me. I realized how much I cared about them—Loydene and U Haul and DeWitt and all the rest. I truly wanted to help them reach that dream they had worked so hard for. How could I confess that I didn't have the faintest idea what to do, then watch the hope fade from all those eyes? And how could I let Thor down without even trying?

Something Dad had said once came back to me: "If you act as if you know what you're doing, people will believe in you." Well, I was about to find out if my acting abilities were that good.

I took a deep breath, pulling in all the confidence I could locate. "Here's what we're going to do," I said, stepping to the center of the room.

What I told them was that I would give the musical cues with my drums. They were all familiar with my introductory beats for each song, and they knew what beat DeWitt came in on. I would also say Thor's lines, since the audience would never know that it was supposed to have been any different. "Just listen closely and watch me when you can," I said. "I'll try to give you all the cues. We're going to put on a terrific show, win or lose—and let's go to win! It's going to be hard without Thor, but we can do it."

U Haul stood up, shooting a fist into the air. "Did you know," he bellowed, "that when the going gets tough, the tough get going?"

Everybody groaned.

"Where did you get *that*?" somebody asked.

"Probably off a Wheaties box," somebody else said. "That's all he ever reads."

That kind of changed the mood, and by the time it

was our turn to go on, everybody was up. I still felt like a total fraud, but I gave the starting drum roll, nodded to DeWitt, and we were off.

The show was fantastic—not a missed cue, not a skipped beat. I knew it wasn't because of me. They were doing it because Thor had inspired them, and they were doing their best for him. They believed in themselves.

We won first place. You'd have thought we'd just won World War II the way everybody cheered and hugged each other when it was announced. I was a rag when it was all over, but at least I could carry good news with me when I went to see Thor the next day.

That night I lay awake, thinking over the day and listening to Blastoff gallop around his corral. He reminded me of the song in *Cats* where beat-up old Grizabella sings about being alone in the moonlight with her memories of her days in the sun. I was happy that Blastoff had had one more day in the sun. Despite what he had done to Thor, I had to admire that arrogant old horse who never let his dreams die. I finally fell asleep, soothed by the rhythm of his thudding hooves. Or was it the memories of my own thumping drums in the prize-winning road show?

I was awakened the next morning by Aunt Adabelle's voice. She was talking to someone in the attic again.

"You old villain," she was saying, "you haven't got me yet. No sirreee, you hollow-eyed old vandal, you're going to have to go some to catch up with Adabelle Spencer."

She sounded the way she did that first day when I came and she was tearing into old Blastoff. If I hadn't known better, I would have thought he was up there in the attic with her. It couldn't be Uncle Vic she was scolding that way. I still wondered who it was she talked with up there.

I didn't go up to find out, though, because it was none of my business, and besides, I wanted to go over and talk to Thor before I ate breakfast. If he was going to yell at me, I didn't want a lump of bacon and eggs churning around in my stomach, making me feel sicker than I already did.

I considered wearing my pioneer dress over to the Jorgensens'. Thor had really liked me in that, and I thought he might not be as mad at me if I reminded him of that night. But this wasn't something I could leave town to escape, like I did the Great Dog-Food Caper. This was something I had to take my lashes for.

I ended up putting on the exact same thing I had been wearing when I first came to Wolf Creek. I figured I might as well end up with Thor the way I began. But just before I left my room, I stood in front of the mirror, took a scissors, and lopped off that tail of purple hair. I don't know why I did it. Maybe just to show that although I was still a dud, I wasn't the same girl I had been when I came.

Outside, the morning was still soft and dewy. The birds were talking to the sun, and the early morning haze hadn't quite cleared away, so the colors of the grass and sky were muted. Maybe that's why the brilliant red of Blastoff's ribbons caught my eye as I passed his corral. Or maybe it was because they contrasted so sharply with the dull brown of the earth where he lay.

I had never seen Blastoff lying down before. I guess I knew even before I saw Bucky sitting silently there in the dirt beside him that he was dead. He lay stretched out under the tall shade tree, as if he'd gone there to rest after his final performance for the shadowy phantoms of the night.

"Oh, no," I whispered. I thought of what it must have been like for Bucky to come find him there.

Quickly I opened the corral gate and went inside, shutting it after me, then wondering why because there was no reason to keep it closed anymore.

I knelt beside Bucky. His head was bent, and he was stroking Blastoff's quiet face.

"Bucky," I said. "Oh, Bucky, I'm so sorry."

He turned, and I saw there had been tears some time before but that they were gone now, leaving dry tracks down his cheeks.

"I'm glad we left his ribbons on," he said. "It makes him look all dressed up."

I had to wait a moment before I could say anything. Then I said, "Did you find him like this?"

Bucky wiped his arm up across his face. "He was already down when I came, but he raised his head and said good-bye. You know how he did. Sort of nickered down deep in his chest. I got down where he could see me and scratched behind his ears the way he liked." Bucky sniffed a couple of times, then went on. "Pretty soon he just . . . went. I closed his eyes for him." He reached out and rearranged the braids of Blastoff's mane so that the ribbons all went neatly in the same direction.

I hugged him, and for a minute he buried his face in my shoulder. Then he pulled away and looked up at me. "Shanny, will you help me bring some flowers for him? He liked those yellow roses across the creek."

We gathered big bouquets of yellow roses and arranged them all around Blastoff. Bucky went into the barn and brought out a faded saddle blanket that had BLASTOFF woven into it. Draping it across the horse's side, he heaped more roses on top.

When we finished, Bucky sat down in the dirt again and stroked the skinny old neck. "When I was a little kid," he said, "I used to pretend that Blastoff would still be around when I got big, and we would go off together to ride in all the rodeos in the world."

"Bucky," I said, "are you okay?"

He nodded without looking up. "I still have the kittens. I have to go up to the Bride's House pretty soon and see if they are all right."

I shouldn't have worried about Bucky. He already knew about the basics of life—birth, death, and caring.

I kissed him on the cheek, then went back to the house. To my surprise, I found that I was crying. I guess I was already thinking of the emptiness of the corral without that crazy old horse running around in it, sneering at the world. There was one gigantic thing wrong with learning to care so much about something, and it was that it hurt so much when you lost it.

Aunt Adabelle was still up in the attic, but she wasn't talking anymore. She was reading some old letters as she sat there in the wicker rocker.

"Come here, Shanny," she said when she saw me. "These are letters your mother and The Cousins sent me a long time . . ." She stopped, peering at my teary face. "Why, what in the world's wrong?"

"Aunt Adabelle," I said, "Blastoff's dead."

"Oh my." She sagged a little in the rocker. "Oh my.

Well, I can't say it's unexpected, but I guess I was hoping it wouldn't come yet."

"Oh, Aunt Adabelle." I stood there blubbering like a big dumb baby. "It's all my fault. If I hadn't talked Thor into riding Blastoff, he wouldn't have been hurt and Blastoff would still be alive. It was just too much for him, all that bucking."

"Oh, pshaw now, Shanny." Aunt Adabelle stood up and put her arms around me. "It's all right. That old horse went out on a real high. That's the way to go, when it's still good." She patted my back as if I were a little kid. "He wouldn't have lasted another winter, Shanny."

"But things are changing so fast," I blubbered, remembering that Aunt Adabelle had said just about the same thing a few days before.

I could feel Aunt Adabelle nodding. "That's true, honey. I was just saying that to myself this morning." She motioned for me to sit in the old wicker rocker, and she sat on a creaky chair beside it.

I sniffled back my tears, wondering how many people had been comforted in that rocker over the years. "Is that who you were talking to this morning, Aunt Adabelle? Yourself?"

Aunt Adabelle chuckled. "No, that was old age I was scolding at. Or maybe death. I don't know. Last night I decided I wasn't going away to any retirement home, and I was just telling whoever might be listening that I wasn't finished yet."

I snuffled again, and Aunt Adabelle pulled an embroidered handkerchief from a box that said Whitman's Chocolates on its top and handed it to me. I wiped my eyes with it. "What happened last night that made you change your mind?"

"*You* happened, Shanny. That's what. I watched you get in there and fight when you didn't think you had anything to fight with. And you came through a winner. I said to myself, 'Adabelle Spencer, if that girl can do it, so can you.' I've watched you these past couple of weeks, and you've got a whale of a lot of grit. I used to have it, too, and I think I've found a little of it left."

I couldn't believe she was talking about *me*. And I didn't fully understand what she was saying. "You mean you're not going to leave the ranch, Aunt Adabelle?"

"No, I'm not. This is my home, Shanny. I'm not going to leave it until I can't get around under my own steam anymore. Oh, I guess you've thought I was ready to be taken away, the way I've been acting." She looked around the attic. "I guess I've been kind of living in the past here with all my old things. But, Shanny, sometimes it's hard to know who you are unless you remember who you were."

"I know, Aunt Adabelle. I know." I squeezed her hand. I had failed again. I wasn't going to get Aunt Adabelle packed off to a retirement home. But somehow I didn't mind at all.

"Would you like me to stay here with you, Aunt Adabelle? I will if you want me to." This time my future with Thor had nothing to do with my desire to stay, since I had no future with Thor.

"That's a right nice offer, Shanny, but you've got a life down there in California that you'll want to take another look at now. Maybe you can come back next summer." She stood up. "No, I'll be all right here alone for a while. I guess I want to be like Blastoff and die in my own corral."

I stood up, too, and we started downstairs. Aunt Adabelle was right, of course. I did have to go back to California. I needed to see Dan and Mom with new eyes. And they needed to see the new me. But which new me? I felt like Shirley's litter of kittens. Maybe I'd just have to line my many selves up in front of my parents and let them take their pick.

But that was a future problem. Right now I had to go face Thor.

He was lying flat on his bed when Mrs. Jorgensen took me to his room. His eyes were closed.

"Go on in, Shanny," Mrs. Jorgensen said. "He's been waiting for you to come. If he needs anything, I'll be downstairs." She turned and left, leaving me alone with Thor.

My heart broke as I stood there looking at him lying pale and helpless on his bed. How he must hate me! I thought again about how painful it was when you cared about something, then lost it. But maybe the caring was worth it. Aunt Adabelle hadn't stopped caring after she lost so many of the things she loved over the years. Maybe the pain was part of it all, part of being alive.

I took a step forward, and Thor opened his eyes. "I knew you'd come dressed like that," he said.

I had come prepared to have him yell at me, or at least chew me out for being the cause of his lying there like that. But here he was, talking about my dumb clothes. "How could you know that?" I stammered.

"Because that's the way you arrived a month ago,

ready to tackle the world from behind that disguise."

Disguise? Were my clothes and haircut nothing more than a costume like my dad's pickle suit, something for me to hide behind? Was I still hiding?

I asked him that. "Am I still hiding?"

He grinned. "It's more of a defense, Shanny. Didn't you come thinking I was going to attack you?"

"You *should* attack me," I burst out. "I did an awful thing to you, making you ride Blastoff. And it's more awful than you know. Thor, Blastoff's dead."

"I already know," Thor said. "Bucky told me about him. He came by on his way to the Bride's House." He winced as he pulled himself to a semi-sitting position against some pillows. "Shanny, you did Blastoff a favor by giving him one last big day. And Bucky told me about what you did there at the corral. The roses and all. It's real nice of you to care so much about a little kid and an old horse."

I was close to tears again. "How could I *not* care about them, Thor? They're some of the best things that have ever happened to me."

Thor nodded. "I know. I know." He shifted again, trying to get comfortable. I guess I must have looked concerned because he said, "Look, Shanny, this is not your fault. I knew what that old horse was like. I got on him of my own free will." He grinned again. "And do you know that I'm glad I did?"

Those tears were almost floating my eyeballs. "Thanks for that, Thor," I said. "I couldn't leave next week thinking you hated me."

He shifted to sit up a little straighter, wincing again. "Shanny, you can't leave at all! What's it going to be like without you here? Dull, that's what it's going to be like."

"Maybe I'll get a couple weeks' extension," I said. "And I'll be back next summer. And did you know I'm a terrific letter-writer?"

Thor's eyes brightened. In fact, he was looking at me just the way I had dreamed that he would someday. It made me so nervous I started babbling. "Did you know," I said, "that the tune of 'Chopsticks' was composed by a sixteen-year-old girl named Euphemia Allen back in 1877? Did you know that the country of Hungary is shaped like a stomach?"

"Shanny," Thor said, "did you know that if I could reach you I would kiss you?"

"Did *you* know," I said, "that it would take me just three short steps to be close enough for you to reach me?"

Thor held out his hand. "So when are you going to take those three steps?"

"Right now," I said. And I did.